Nothing less than a Hollywood romance would do . . .

Alice is calm, cool, and aloof—except for the night she meets her new neighbor Dr. Nicholas Bale—aka Hot Doc. The chemistry between them might be through the roof but that doesn't mean she's going to let him into her life. Having been seen at her most vulnerable, she vows to have nothing to do with the sexy doctor. After all, Alice learned long ago that love only leads to hurt.

Nicholas is smitten at first sight with the gorgeous, mysterious redhead upstairs. But between her attempts to push him away and the even bigger wall around her heart, the dashing doctor is having a hard time getting close to the sensitive beauty. Then he glimpses the emotion in her eyes as she watches Fred and Ginger whirl across the screen and he's determined to uncover just what it will take to dance his way in to her heart . . .

Visit us at www.kensingtonbooks.com

I0677620

Books by Maggie Dallen

The Chance Series
The Accidental Engagement
The Accidental Boyfriend
The Accidental Elopement

Reel Romance Series
Her Leading Man
His Leading Lady

Published by Kensington Publishing Corporation

His Leading Lady

A Reel Romance

Maggie Dallen

LYRICAL PRESS
Kensington Publishing Corp.
www.kensingtonbooks.com

Lyrical Press books are published by

Kensington Publishing Corp. 119 West 40th Street New York, NY 10018

Copyright © 2017 by Maggie Dallen

All Kensington titles, imprints, and distributed lines are available at special quantity discounts for bulk purchases for sales promotion, premiums, fund-raising, and educational or institutional use.

Special book excerpts or customized printings can also be created to fit specific needs. For details, write or phone the office of the Kensington Special Sales Manager:
Kensington Publishing Corp.
119 West 40th Street
New York, NY 10018
Attn. Special Sales Department. Phone: 1-800-221-2647.

Kensington and the K logo Reg. U.S. Pat. & TM Off.
Lyrical Press and the L logo are trademarks of Kensington Publishing Corp.

First Electronic Edition: July 2017
eISBN-13: 978-1-5161-0142-9
eISBN-10: 1-5161-0142-1

First Print Edition: July 2017
ISBN-13: 978-1-5161-0145-0
ISBN-10: 1-5161-0145-6

Printed in the United States of America

Chapter 1

Alice was once again faced with the daily showdown—between two pairs of shoes. She sank back in her office chair and contemplated the contents of her bottom drawer. One high-heeled and strappy—perfect for a night out on the town—the other her cozy, well-worn flats, which practically begged her to slip them on and walk home.

Her big meeting with the boss was over, everyone else in the midtown public relations office of Jamison & Co. had left for the day, and she should be out celebrating. But those flats looked so much more appealing.

Her phone chimed with a new text. *Ugh, Bradley.*

"Hey, babe, we on for tonight?"

No, Bradley. Just no. No for so many reasons. "Babe"? Really? Who does he think he was, an action star from the eighties? But mainly because she and Bradley went on date number three two nights ago and, while he may not know it yet, he'd maxed out. She had a strict three-date policy, and she certainly wasn't going to be bending any rules for Bradley "Hey, babe" Newton.

She picked up the phone and texted back. "Sorry, made other plans."

And like that it was decided. The comfy shoes won. Shoving the sexy heels back into their drawer, she slipped on the flats and headed home.

The walk from her office to her Upper West Side apartment was more than a mile, but it gave her a chance to decompress after a long, albeit successful, day. She stopped off at the corner store to pick up a pint of mint chocolate chip ice cream before heading to her high-rise apartment building on Riverside. The doorman, Carl, gave her a nod of greeting.

The doorman and the view—that was what had sold her on her current studio apartment. *Luxury* studio, her realtor had liked to stress. And it was luxurious, but only because of the doorman and the epic, sweeping view of the Hudson and the Jersey skyline. Other than that it was just your basic studio.

She took the elevator up to her floor, let herself in to her *luxury* studio, and swapped out her form-fitting skirt suit for some oversized flannel pajamas and a pair of fuzzy slippers. After throwing her long red hair up into a haphazard topknot, she grabbed the ice cream off the counter, and took the stairs down three flights.

Ena answered on the second knock, her white frizzy hair a halo around her wrinkled, smiling face. "Alice!" she cried, as if Alice's presence on her doorstep was a great surprise and not a frequent event.

Alice thrust the ice cream at her old neighbor. "I come bearing gifts."

Ena chuckled as she took the ice cream and held the door open for Alice to enter. "What's the special occasion?" Her eyes widened with excitement. "Did you get the promotion?"

"No." She walked into the woman's one-bedroom apartment, which miraculously always seemed to smell like something was baking. "Not yet," she added quickly. It was just a matter of time. Alice did not take no for an answer, not when she really wanted something. And this promotion—she deserved it. None of the other junior associates worked as hard as she did. The senior associate job was hers. She just needed her boss to make it official.

Alice headed straight toward Ena's DVD collection, which lined a bookshelf that covered most of one wall in her friend's living room.

"So what's this big news?" Ena called out from the kitchen.

Alice studied the lineup of old movies, skimming over the westerns and the film noirs. Tonight was a celebration, which called for—aha! She reached out and snatched *Swing Time* from where it was wedged between *Easter Parade* and *The Maltese Falcon*.

Ena came out of the kitchen, two bowls of ice cream in hand and handed one to Alice. "The news?" she prompted as they both took their usual seats on their respective love seats.

Alice grinned at her friend. "I got my boss to agree to my pro bono plan."

Ena tipped her head down and looked up at her with raised brows.

"Oh, okay, *our* pro bono plan."

Her friend smiled at that and leaned back against the couch, digging in to her ice cream. "So the big boss will let you take on The Ellen for free, huh? What kind of PR campaign do you have in mind?"

The Ellen was the old movie theater downtown that had fallen into disrepair. Alice, her sister, Meg, and her husband, Jake, along with some other friends, were part of the volunteer crew who went to the theater every other Saturday morning to do whatever fix-up work they could. Since none of them were in the construction field, that typically meant cleaning, painting, and other non-substantial handyman work that needed to be done.

Alice leaned forward, her ice cream temporarily forgotten in her excitement. "A costume party," she said. "With my company's sponsorship, I want to throw a party at the theater and everyone will come dressed as their favorite classic movie star or character."

She waited expectantly; her body was still on edge with excitement. There was nothing she loved more than starting up a new PR campaign for a new client—and to have that client be as near and dear to her heart as The Ellen? It was too good to be true.

Ena's answering excitement didn't disappoint. The old woman's face lit up with a smile. "Sounds perfect!" Her eyes narrowed a bit with suspicion. "It also sounds like the perfect way to earn brownie points with your Mr. Dixon."

Alice laughed. "You caught me." So maybe it wasn't quite as selfless as she'd made it sound. She did want to help The Ellen—of course she did—but it didn't hurt that her immediate boss, the one responsible for handing out the promotions, had mentioned more than once how beneficial some good pro bono projects would be for the company's image. Most of the junior associates loathed pro bono work—Alice included—since a good portion of their salary came from commissions and bonuses, which were a guaranteed zero if you took on a free project. But, Alice had been raking in the money these past few years, what she needed now was a promotion. Once she got that, more money would come her way. The problem with her junior colleagues is that they couldn't see the long-term picture—they didn't have an end goal in mind.

But not Alice. She smirked at her friend. "Is there anything wrong with having my cake and eating it, too?"

Ena laughed and shook her head. "Not at all, dear. So, when are you going to tell the others?" Her voice held more than a hint of mockery as she added, "Team *Operation Petticoat*."

Operation Petticoat was the name their little group of volunteers had given themselves, based on the old movie in which a motley crew salvages an old, badly damaged submarine. Ena thought the name was hopelessly cheesy. Alice had tried to explain that it had been Caitlyn's idea—one of her friends in the crew, Caitlyn was beyond obsessed with Cary Grant, so of course she'd come up with a name that was also the title of one of his movies. While Ena could respect the Cary Grant adoration, she had a thing against Tony Curtis, the co-star of that particular Cary Grant comedy.

"Our next meet up is this Saturday morning," Alice said, ignoring the jibe at the name. "I figure I can wait a day to tell them so I can see their reactions in person."

Although, shifting in her seat with excitement, Alice started to reconsider that plan. They would all be so excited, particularly Tamara, her friend who ran the old theater. Since the owner didn't seem to care what happened to the place, it fell on Tamara's slim shoulders to try to get the theater on the city's list of historical landmarks. So far she'd had no success—but an elegant gala for some of Manhattan's wealthiest and most influential was sure to help. If nothing else, the publicity would make it harder for the owner to sell the property and have it turned into condos or a mall or a something, which seemed to be his most recent plan.

"Maybe I should call Tamara," she said.

Ena stood from the couch. "I'll make us some tea while you talk to your friend. And then…" She leaned over and picked up the movie where Alice had set it on the coffee table. "I see it's a Fred and Ginger night, eh?"

Alice shrugged. "I was in the mood."

Ena gave a little snort of laughter. She knew very well that Fred and Ginger's flicks were Alice's go-to feel-good movies. She was pretty much always in the mood for them. Every once in a while they shook things up with a screwball comedy or a classic drama, but more often than not, when Alice showed up at Ena's door, she was either there for some comfort, which called for a feel-good movie, or to celebrate—which also called for a feel-good movie.

"Surprise, surprise," Ena said. She straightened up and one hand flew to her chest, her already pale face blanching.

Alice leaned forward. "Ena? Are you all right?"

The tension eased out of her friend's body, and she gave Alice a smile as she waved off her concern. "It's nothing. Just indigestion."

Ena headed to the kitchen to make tea, and Alice searched around her for her phone so she could give Tamara the good news. She frowned at the empty space on the couch beside her and the coffee table, which was covered in knickknacks but no phone. Muttering a curse, she realized she'd left it on the kitchen counter of her own apartment. Apparently in her rush to get down to her friend's apartment, she'd forsaken her phone but remembered the always-crucial ice cream. After all, movie night wouldn't be movie night without that.

She called out to Ena, who was still in the kitchen. "Mind if I borrow your phone for a quick call?"

"Go ahead, dear."

Alice reached for the cell phone that she'd bought her friend as a Hanukkah present two years before. Ena had held onto the notion that a landline was good enough for her, but Alice had insisted that someone of her age—which was well into her eighties, although Ena refused to say her exact age—should have a phone handy at all times just in case, so she'd bought her one, and Ena had finally gotten rid of her landline.

She found the prepaid phone on an end table and scowled at the device when it refused to turn on. "Ena, when's the last time you charged this thing?"

Ena didn't answer, though Alice was well aware her friend could hear her. She may be elderly, but there was nothing wrong with her hearing.

Rolling her eyes, she abandoned the dead phone to search for the charger. "What's the use of having an emergency phone if it doesn't work?"

Ena came out of the kitchen carrying two empty mugs and a sugar bowl. Setting them down on the coffee table she ignored the phone comment and placed her hands on her hips. "Tell me, Alice, what are you doing here celebrating with me when you should be out with that nice young man. What was his name…Bradley?"

Alice stilled, one hand buried in the drawer that held all kinds of random items, not one of which appeared to be a charger. She smiled up at her friend with as much sweetness and innocence as she could muster. Sweet and innocent were not exactly her forte, so she wasn't surprised when Ena let out a snort of disbelief.

"What?" Alice said. "I'd rather spend time with one of my dearest friends. Is that so wrong?"

"Ha!" Ena's laugh held no humor. "Poor Bradley hit date three, didn't he?"

Alice dropped the sweet smile and gave a shrug. "You know the rule."

Ena rolled her eyes. "Your rules are stupid."

Holding back a sigh, Alice pretended to be absorbed in searching Ena's end table drawer for the charger. The last thing she wanted was to hear this lecture again. But ignoring her friend did nothing to stop her. "You're too young to be so cynical."

Alice did sigh then. This was how every lecture started. She was too young to be cynical. But honestly, Alice had been cynical since the age of eleven when her father took off. Her cynicism had only grown since then, growing more ingrained with every one of her mother's disastrous relationships.

"You should be out there dating, falling in love…" Ena was saying.

Alice tuned her out. She'd gotten good at doing that. The lecture would end soon enough, once Ena ran out of steam.

Hopping up off the couch, she temporarily gave up on finding the charger. She took a couple steps toward the kitchen. "Need a hand in there?" she asked. "Here, let me get that teakettle for you, the water should be done by now."

Ena hustled toward the kitchen to cut her off, as Alice had known she would. She may be predictable with her love of old musicals, but Ena was even more so. She was territorial to the extreme about her kitchen. No one was allowed in there but her.

"Oh no you don't," she said, cutting Alice off at the doorway. Making a shooing motion, she waved Alice back.

She was heading back to the living room to continue her hunt for a charger when she heard a loud clattering sound from the kitchen. Spinning on her heel she raced into the forbidden room.

Her blood froze in her veins at the sight of Ena on the floor clutching her chest. She raced over to her side and saw the older woman's face screwed up in pain.

9-1-1. Have to call 9-1-1. Panic had Alice's hands shaking as she looked around the room for help. There was the old landline phone, which no longer worked. Her phone was upstairs, and Ena's phone was dead.

Shit. This could not be happening.

Squeezing Ena's hand, she said, "I'll be right back with help."

She raced out of the apartment and to the staircase so she could run to her apartment and call for an ambulance. But then, as if on cue, the elevator doors pinged open in front of her. *Elevator. Yes, quicker.* She darted for it and collided face-first into the man who was exiting the elevator.

Strong arms caught her but the full force of the contact had her winded. Still, she managed to get out, "Doctor. I need a doctor."

* * * *

Dr. Nicholas Bale's night started off bad and ended up so much worse.

He'd started his night at his best friend's loft apartment in Tribeca. He and Claudia stood side by side as the last of her dinner party guests left. He was the last one standing, aside from her husband, Frank, who was in the kitchen loading the dishwasher.

A smile still plastered onto his face, Nicholas gave a little wave to the cute blonde who turned to give him one last brilliant smile before she got on the elevator.

The moment the doors closed, Nicholas let the fake smile fall, and he heard Claudia sigh beside him. "Entertaining is exhausting," she said as they both took a step back into the apartment so she could shut the door, officially declaring an end to the dinner, which had been a well-staged but barely veiled setup attempt.

"You're the one who keeps insisting on throwing these little parties," he reminded her.

She shrugged helplessly, making her black spiral curls bounce against her shoulders. "I know. I guess I'm just a glutton for punishment."

"Or a shameless matchmaker."

"Guilty." Her smile was shameless as she led the way back to the loft's spacious den. They both fell back into the oversized couch with a sigh. Classical music still played softly in the background, and the soft clinking sound of dishes in the kitchen was a homey, comforting backdrop.

The fact that he could finally relax for the first time all night—and after a killer shift in the pediatrics ward—had him nearly ready to doze off on that comfy couch.

"Admit it," Claudia said. "Helen was a pretty good choice."

Nicholas nodded. "She was...lovely." And she was. His blind date had been everything he'd told Claudia he wanted—warm, witty, and kind. And empirically speaking, she was pretty, no doubt about it.

Claudia's head dropped back against the couch as she groaned. "Uh oh."

"What?"

She turned her head to face him. "You hesitated. Why, what's wrong with her?"

Nicholas opened his mouth to speak and then closed it. Nothing. Nothing was wrong with her. He just hadn't felt *it*—a spark, or a connection—whatever it was that was supposed to be the dead giveaway when you met *the one* or a viable contender for *the one*, at least.

Claudia was still watching him, and her face fell at whatever she saw in his expression. "Seriously, Nick. What was wrong with her? This is the third woman I've set you up with this month, and you haven't liked any of them. How can you expect me to find you a nice girl if you don't give me some feedback?"

Nicholas winced. She was right—he'd been a difficult matchmaking client, to say the least. And it wasn't like he was unwilling. About six months ago he'd made the decision that he was finally ready to settle down. He'd gotten to a stable position at the hospital and was ready to focus on the next step of his life plan. Marriage, kids...the whole white-picket-fence scenario. It was time. And if there was one thing Nicholas excelled at it was creating life goals and attaining them. This should be no different. But months passed and he'd had no success—between his busy work schedule and his small social network, finding a wife the old-fashioned way had not been fruitful.

He'd gone to his best friend with the problem, and she'd been ecstatic to hear that he was finally open to being set up on blind dates—something she'd been trying to push on him since they'd studied premed together at college. She'd even managed to convince him to try his hand at online dating, but his few attempts to date had been spectacular failures.

Claudia was still waiting for a response, but he had none to give. "I think you don't know what you want," she finally said.

She might as well have slapped him in the face. Straightening his shoulders, he gave her his haughtiest look. "That is not true. I've told you exactly what I want."

"Right," Claudia laughed. "Miss Perfect. Well, I hate to break this to you, *Hot Doc*, but the perfect woman does not exist."

He ignored her use of the nickname she'd given him in college—the one he hated with a passion. "I'm not looking for perfection, but I do think compatibility is important. Like what you have with Frank or what my parents had when they were alive."

Claudia looked down her nose at him. "I have a feeling you're glorifying your parents' romance. And I *know* you're doing it to mine. Lord knows I love my husband, but we are so far from perfect." Though he was safely in the kitchen and out of earshot, she called out, "No offense, honey!"

Nicholas didn't bother to argue. She didn't get it—he wasn't looking for perfection, he was looking for…simple. Easy companionship. He didn't need some torrid affair or a passionate emotional relationship—he was looking for a teammate, a friend to share a life with.

"I don't think it's crazy to be looking for a woman who shares the same goals, the same dreams for the future."

Claudia gave a short laugh. "Not everyone is as goal-oriented as you are, my friend. Most of us are just making it up as we go along." Before he could respond, she switched the topic. "So Helen wasn't the girl of your dreams. Duly noted. I'll keep looking. In the meantime, how's online dating going?"

Nicholas cringed at the memory of his last date. A girl who'd seemed perfect on paper but when he met her had turned out to be something else entirely. Her whole profile was devoted to how much she wanted a long-term commitment, then when he showed up she informed him that her roommate had actually made her profile and it was all one big lie.

"So far it's been a waste of time."

Claudia murmured something about kissing a lot of frogs, which made him laugh. "Thanks for the wise words of wisdom, Claudia, but I can't waste time on someone who doesn't want the same things as me."

He could practically feel his best friend roll her eyes. "Oh right, I forgot, you're on a timeline."

She made it sound like it was the worst thing in the world. But really, he hadn't gotten where he was—a highly successful, renowned pediatric surgeon at a world-class hospital—without having a plan. And plans required a timeline and end goals.

Finding his wife and future mother of his children was no different.

"My timeline is perfectly reasonable. Now is the perfect time to find my partner. If I get this promotion—"

"*When* you get it," Claudia chimed in supportively.

"If I get it, I'll be relocating and—"

"Yeah, yeah," Claudia cut in. "Now is the perfect time to meet your wife. I've heard this all before. I just think that perhaps you're being too narrow-minded about this perfect woman of yours."

Nicholas shrugged. They'd been through this before. "I know what I want."

"You always do," she muttered.

He looked over in surprise. "What does that mean?"

Her sigh sounded weary and she sank even farther into the couch as she kicked off her shoes. "I don't think you'll know what you want until it's right in front of your face. And if you want my opinion? It's probably not going to be what you think it is."

Nicholas turned to her with a frown. He was a man who got what he set his mind to; Claudia knew that better than anyone. "What makes you say that?"

She turned to face him then and her smile was enigmatic, like she was laughing at a joke she wouldn't share. "Because that's the way love works, Hot Doc. It couldn't care less about your plans."

Nicholas had no response to that—he had little to no experience with love in his own life, he'd never had time for that particular adventure, so he was hardly in a position to argue. Ceding temporary defeat, he pushed himself off the couch and pulled Claudia up along with him so he could give her a hug and say his good-byes.

Frank came out of the kitchen to shake his hand and when Nicholas got onto the elevator he turned back for one last good-bye to find his favorite couple friends standing with their arms around one another, leaning against each other in their exhaustion.

A brief pang shot through his chest. *That.* That right there was what he wanted. Despite his friend's cynical words, he found seeing her with her husband was more heartening than anything. True love was out there. His parents had found it and so had his best friend. He was happy for her—she deserved it. Still, seeing his friend's perfect relationship made him that much more aware of what he was missing, and he found himself pushing the button to close the elevator doors so he could escape the sight. "Good night," he called as the doors started to slide shut.

"We'll keep looking," Claudia called out. "Don't give up hope!"

Her words rang in his ears long after the doors shut. Claudia might tease him mercilessly, but she was also his biggest cheerleader. She was also ruthlessly persistent. He had no doubt she would continue weeding through all her available single friends and acquaintances until she found *the one*. Her devotion was sweet, but at that particular moment the thought of facing endless dinners like the one he'd been on tonight made him slouch against the elevator wall with a weary groan.

His parents and Claudia had made finding a life partner look so easy, but so far his search had been fruitless and tiring. For quite possibly the first time in his life, he'd set out to accomplish a task and was failing. Well, maybe it was too soon to call it a failure, but it certainly wasn't coming easily. Perhaps it was time to rethink his strategy. Maybe he should put his wife-hunt on hold, wait until the promotion was a sure thing... But then that would mean delaying his plans.

And life plans waited for no man.

* * * *

Heavy exhaustion weighed on him as he rode in a taxi uptown to his Riverside high-rise apartment building. He gave the doorman a quick nod as he got in the elevator.

Sleep, that was what he needed. His apartment and his bed were calling to him. He needed to shut his mind off for a few blissful hours. The doors slid open with a ding. For just a little while he could turn off all thoughts of work or dating or—

Oof. The force of a woman slamming into his body at a full run temporarily knocked the wind out him. Instinctively holding on to her to keep them both from falling over, there was a stunned moment when he found himself in an odd embrace. One minute he'd been alone on an elevator, and then he was in a hallway, pressed up against a woman.

A gorgeous woman.

She pulled back to look up at him, her eyes impossibly wide and startlingly green. Not emerald green but some shade between green and blue. A turquoise maybe. Her red hair was pulled up off her neck, and her lush lips were parted, like they were begging to be kissed.

He had to be dreaming—the world tilted on its axis as he stared down into the face of the woman. His woman. He'd found her....

But then words rushed out of her mouth, and he was jolted back to reality.

"Doctor. I need a doctor."

Chapter 2

When the stranger spoke, Alice had the unnerving sensation that she was hallucinating.

The blindingly handsome man looked a bit like an angel, and his deep voice was a soothing balm, cutting through her frantic panic. "I'm a doctor."

"You're a doctor?" she repeated. What were the odds that in her hour of need, she would run smack into a doctor sent from heaven? But then the panic returned in full force and the dizzying fear held her in its grip once more. Taking the doctor by the hand, she pulled him toward Ena's apartment.

"Ambulance," she thought she said. "Collapsed. Have to get to hospital." Disjointed words came out of her mouth in a jumble, but the doctor snapped into action with a cool professionalism that was slightly reassuring.

Thank God someone was here who knew what the hell to do.

When they reached Ena, she was still on the floor, but she was conscious. As Alice rushed to her side, she was dimly aware that the doctor was on the phone giving orders, then he was by her side doing all the doctorly things she'd seen on TV but would never have thought to do herself. Checking Ena's pulse, asking her questions, reassuring the patient...and Alice in the process.

The next hour flew by in a blur as an ambulance arrived and paramedics showed up in the apartment with a stretcher. Through it all she was dimly aware of the doctor taking the lead, with Ena and with her.

He led her by the elbow to the ambulance and helped her into the back so she could stay with Ena. He went to close the door, and terror had her gripping his arm like he was a lifeline. And he was. He was the only thing that seemed to make any sense in this nightmare of a night.

He stopped and covered her hand with his. "I'll be right behind you."

Gently uncurling her clenched fingers, he closed the door.

She paced the waiting room for what felt like hours, anxiety churning alongside a stomach full of terrible hospital coffee. The caffeine made her edgy on top of being worried out of her mind. Her deep-seated fear of hospitals wasn't helping anything either. She fought off the bad memories that threatened to drown her, but the fear seemed to live in her bones and the seeped into her blood. The stranger who'd accompanied her to the hospital had sat with her for a while, which had helped a little. He didn't force her to talk, and for that she'd been grateful. But then, as impatient as she was to get word on Ena's condition, he'd told her he was going to track down the doctor on duty to get an update.

She'd briefly considered calling her sister to keep her company while she waited, but Meg was ready to pop with pregnancy—she needed her sleep. There was no one else she felt comfortable calling. She had friends, of course, but no one she could turn to in a crisis.

That's what you get for being so stubbornly independent. She could practically hear Ena's voice in her head, chastising her. Ena was always giving her a hard time for being too closed off for not trusting enough. What Ena didn't understand—had never understood—was that trusting people was not easy for her. She didn't know how people did it. She trusted Meg and Ena. That was it.

Oh God, please don't let anything happen to Ena. That woman was the closest thing to a grandmother she'd ever known, and over the past few years she'd been more of a motherly figure than her own mother had ever been.

By the time the double doors swung open, she was ready to jump out of her skin.

It was *him*—the doctor from earlier in the night, the one who'd miraculously appeared when she'd needed him most. Beside him was a young bald man wearing scrubs—the ER doctor on duty, she guessed.

"How is she?" Alice asked, her hands wrapping and unwrapping around the now-cold coffee cup in her hands.

The bald doctor frowned at her. "You're Ms. Knight's granddaughter?"

She nodded quickly. She'd almost forgotten that lie she'd told the nurse who'd made it clear that only relatives would be informed of the patient's condition.

"She'll live."

Alice let out a long breath. Relief coursed through her. She was grateful that the doctor hadn't beaten around the bush and had told her what she needed to hear first.

The hot doctor—*her* doctor, as she was starting to think of him —took her gently by the elbow and steered her toward a seat. She sank into it, and he took the seat beside her as the ER doctor filled her in on the details. Ena had suffered a heart attack, it seemed. Not life-threatening thanks to the quick response time, but serious enough that they were keeping her for observation for the next few days.

Alice nodded as he spoke, trying to register the words as they filtered through her hazy brain. After the rush of adrenaline, followed by the overwhelming wave of relief at the good news, Alice was wrung out—emotionally and physically. His words barely made sense because all she could focus on was one thought—Ena was going to live. She wasn't going to lose her friend.

A choking sensation had her scrambling for breath. She saw the doctor's eyes narrow in on her expression with a look of concern. "Are you all right, miss?"

No. What the hell was this? Her throat was closing up and her eyes were burning. What the... Was she about to cry? No. Impossible. She couldn't. She wouldn't. She hadn't cried since she was nine years old, not even when she'd broken an ankle in volleyball. She sure as hell was not going to cry here, now, in front of a complete stranger.

But even as she thought it, tears came trickling out of her eyes and her breath hitched in her throat in a quiet, gasping sob.

Neither doctor seemed unperturbed by the sudden choking sobs and the stream of tears that were coursing down her cheeks. The ER doctor gave her a sympathetic wince of a smile before heading back through the double doors. As for her doctor, by his calm, cool, composed features and the way he instantly, almost instinctively reached out an arm to wrap around her supportively, it was easy to believe that he was used to seeing women break down every day of the week. And maybe he did. He was a doctor after all, maybe waiting room hysterics were par for the course.

But Alice was *horrified.* Swiping at the errant tears, she found herself trying to get words out through the sobs. "I-I'm s-sorry," she managed. "I d-don't—I n-never c-c-c—"

He interrupted her with a tight squeeze. "It's all right. You have nothing to be sorry about. It's been a trying night."

Alice resisted the tug at first, but his arm felt so good around her shoulders and his broad chest looked so inviting, she gave in with a little wail, letting herself collapse against him as the sobs racked her body, leaving her shaken and exhausted.

She was vaguely aware of the fact that he was murmuring soft words of comfort as he stroked her arm in a rhythmic, soothing motion. The movement lulled her, and his body heat warmed her chilled body. And the scent of him—something earthy and masculine—made her feel safe and cozy. The tears subsided after a little while, but Alice found she didn't have the energy to pull away. Not just yet…

* * * *

Holy shit! Alice sat up with a start, instantly awake and filled with a sinking sensation. She'd fallen asleep. On the stranger's chest, no less. She turned to him, certain that embarrassment had turned her face a special shade of crimson, one typically reserved for cranberries and stop signs.

He smiled at her. Smiled! Like strange women fell asleep on him all the time. No big whoop. Just another day in the life of Doctor Sexy. And holy crap was he sexy. She'd started to think that maybe she'd been hallucinating in the hallway when she'd thought he was an angel sent from above. But now, she knew she hadn't been exaggerating anything in her distress.

This man was beautiful—there was no other way to describe him. Beautiful in a manly way, of course, but beautiful nonetheless. His light brown hair was cut short in a sort of military style, and his features were the stuff of sculptures. His jaw looked like it had been chiseled from stone, and his nose and cheekbones had the sleek lines of an aristocrat. He had vivid blue eyes that seemed to be filled with warmth at all times—whether he was issuing commands to paramedics or cuddling a stranger while she cried.

Maybe warm eyes were a requisite attribute for doctors. Maybe that was all part of the bedside manner thing.

It was then that she realized that she was staring. He didn't seem to mind, he was still giving her that small, comforting smile—the type one might bestow on a small child or a dotty old aunt.

It hit her again—*she'd fallen asleep on him.* For how long? Oh crap, was she drooling? She lifted a hand and wiped the back of her mouth just to be sure.

"Do you want to go see your grandmother?"

She blinked at him, the words not registering. Her grandmother. *Her grandmother?*

Ena! Scrambling to move away from him, she jumped out of her seat. "Yes! Definitely yes. I'd love that." She was rambling but couldn't bring herself to care. Why not add one more bit of crazy to the boatload she'd already dumped on this man.

He led the way through the doors and into the intensive care unit, holding her arm as if he was afraid she might collapse or something. And he had every right to think that given the way she'd just acted, she reminded herself.

Still, she resisted the urge to jerk her arm away. She did *not* need his help. But she let him lead her because despite the fact that she hated his support, she wasn't altogether steady on her feet. The hospital smells were overwhelming, threatening to choke her or make her sick. God, she really hated this place.

He left her at the door, and she didn't turn to say good-bye or thank you in her eagerness to reach Ena's side. She looked like she was sleeping so Alice took the seat at her bedside and settled in, ready to wait it out as long as it took.

It only took two minutes. Ena opened her eyes, which looked extra dark against her paper-white skin and hair. "You're here."

"Of course I'm here. Where else would I be?"

Ena's voice sounded weaker than normal, but she didn't miss a beat. "Oh I don't know, off with a certain hunky doctor?"

Despite the fact that she looked like she'd just narrowly escaped death and was currently lying on a hospital bed, Ena's eyes were filled with mischief.

Alice ignored her. "How are you feeling? Can I get you anything?"

"No, no." She waved off Alice's concern. "I'm fine, and the doctors gave me some medicine that's making it hard to stay awake."

"Then get some sleep, you need your rest." Alice leaned over and pulled the covers up farther and then gave them a little pat to smooth them flat, mainly because it seemed like that was the sort of thing one was supposed to do at a sick person's bedside. But really, she had no idea. The simple gesture felt awkward. She wasn't the mothering nursemaid type—that was Meg's role. She should have had her sister come down here, she would have known what to do...

Ena broke into her thoughts. "You look like you need rest more than I do. Good God, girl, what happened to you?"

Alice spun around to face a mirror on the far side of the room and gave a little shriek at the sight she saw there. Her face was ashen white where it wasn't red and blotchy from crying. Any makeup had been lost in the deluge of tears, and the hair that had at one point been pulled back in a bun was now sticking out and frizzing out all over the place, making her look like a mad scientist.

To top it all off, she was still wearing the ridiculous, oversized pajamas that made her figure look like a giant lump. She was a large potato in a flannel sack.

Her hands came up to her face as she breathed out string of curse words.

Unbelievable. She'd actually let herself be seen like this. In public. By *him*. She had a vivid memory of sobbing onto the nice doctor's shirt, and an irrational anger swept through her. Some stranger had seen her cry. And not just any stranger—a hot guy.

Alice did not cry, and she sure as hell didn't lose her cool in front of strange, hot men. She just didn't.

Her blotchy face was a rude reminder that yes, apparently she did.

It was a onetime thing. An anomaly. She inhaled deeply and squared her shoulders. It would never happen again.

Ena's voice broke into her inner tirade. "So? What do you think of that doctor? He's right up your alley."

She gaped at her reflection in the mirror before spinning around to face Ena. "Are you kidding? Doctor vanilla ice cream?" She feigned a yawn. "Too boring for my tastes. Besides, he probably has a perfect little wife and two-point-five kids waiting for him in the suburbs." Her reflection frowned back at her as her brain summoned up an image of the sexy doctor with his perfect wife on his arm. She'd bet money the woman in question was a blond bombshell—elegant, sleek, and disgustingly sweet.

Ena's soft laugh had her shaking off the nauseating mental image as she turned to face her friend.

"Methinks thou doth protest too much."

Alice rolled her eyes, but a tightness in her chest eased at the sight of her friend's smile, which was as lively as ever despite her wan features. "He's not my type."

"Why? Because he's seen you like this?" She pointed to Alice's wardrobe and let out a cackling laugh. "You just don't like him because he's seen you vulnerable. I can read you like a book."

Alice ignored her as she settled into the chair once more. "So are you going to sleep, or are you going to keep harassing me?"

Ena's lips clamped shut but she looked like she was smothering a smile. She shut her eyes, and Alice let out a sigh of relief that the conversation was over. She was ready to head home, take a shower, and forget all about the awful image of Ena on the ground. And the humiliating image of her utter loss of dignity in front of the sexy doctor.

But then Ena said, "I can ask him if he's single if you'd like."

Alice groaned. She should have known Ena wouldn't give up that easily—even when she was doped up and in pain. Her friend was bound and determined to find Alice a love match, despite the fact that Alice didn't do love.

"Good night, Ena," she said as she gathered her purse and headed toward the door.

"One date with the dashing doctor," Ena called after her.

Alice paused in the doorway long enough to say, "I plan on never seeing the dashing doctor again as long as I live. Now go get some sleep."

She'd left the room and had taken two steps toward the exit when she heard Ena call out after her, "But you do admit he's dashing!"

* * * *

Alice pushed a broom across the lobby of The Ellen on a chilly Saturday morning and lamented her fate. "I am single-handedly saving this theater, and you're still putting me on gum duty? This is so unfair."

Tamara, who was following behind her with a mop, gave a little snort of a laugh. The petite blonde had her long mane of hair piled up on top of her head while she cleaned, making her look even more like a ballerina than usual—like she might break into a pirouette at any moment. "The gala is an awesome idea, Alice, but let's not get ahead of ourselves. The owner is still looking for a buyer, and I've still had no word back from the historical preservation people about whether or not we qualify for landmark status."

Tamara ran the theater and had the most to lose if the owner sold the place. She, like the others, had been ecstatic when Alice broke the news about the new company-sponsored theme party in two weeks, but Alice couldn't fault the girl for keeping her expectations low. She was the one working the hardest to keep this place going and had the most to lose if they failed.

Meg waddled over to her, her big baby belly leading the way as she handed Alice the dreaded gum scraper. "Caitlyn took off early—"

"To meet her *luv-uh,* " Marc, Tamara's roommate, called out.

Meg rolled her eyes. "Yes, most likely to meet Ben." To Alice she added, "Which means you're up for gum duty."

Alice narrowed her eyes at her sister. No one wanted gum duty—ever. "You just love bossing us all around, don't you?"

Since she was nearly nine months along in her pregnancy, Meg had become less and less active in the cleaning and more and more of a drill sergeant with the to-do list.

Meg's eyes were sparkling with humor. With her short brown curls and pixie features, she looked like a mischievous elf. "It's not the worst job."

"No, that would be gum duty," she grumbled. Meg's lips clamped shut as she smothered a laugh. Alice sighed melodramatically as she took the scraper. "You're gonna be a mean mommy." Since Meg had all but raised her, they both knew that wasn't true, and her sister's laughter followed her as she stalked past her through the double doors that led to the opulent, if tattered, theater.

There was a part of her—a very little part—that was grateful for the dreaded task. Scraping gum off the theater seats meant being alone in the theater. She'd called in sick on Friday and slept most of the day away. This morning she'd woken up in a funk, as if her brain hadn't fully processed everything that had happened on Thursday night.

When she'd arrived this morning she'd told her friends all about the pro bono gig but left out the part about Ena and the hospital. But it was all she could think about. How frail her friend had looked lying on the floor, how useless she'd been in the face of trauma, and how incredibly useful the doctor had been.

The doctor—that's what it all kept coming back to. His eyes, his warmth, the solid weight of him against her cheek. *As she cried all over him.*

Disgust had her scraping the seats with enough force that her arm started to ache. Ridiculous or not, a growing resentment had formed whenever she pictured his face. He'd seen her *cry*, for God's sake.

But it was fine, she reassured herself as she brushed back her hair and sat back on her heels to appraise her work. She would never see him again.

That thought just brought up another line of questioning that had driven her crazy the day before. *Where had he come from?*

If she didn't have such a vivid memory of his scent and feel, she might have thought she'd conjured him up. She'd never seen him before at her Riverside apartment building—and he was a man she would have noticed.

Maybe he was there to visit a friend.

That thought put her at ease a bit.

And what were the odds that he was a doctor at the hospital where Ena was staying? Slim to none. He'd just said he was a doctor, not where he worked or what type.

Gum scraping turned out to be a therapeutic event. By the time she was done, she'd convinced herself that if she hadn't seen the handsome doctor before, odds were she would never see him again.

The whole crying debacle was behind her forever. Now if she could just forget about the whole embarrassing incident, she could move on with her life.

Meg popped her head in to say good-bye a little while later. "You going back to the hospital?" she asked.

Alice nodded. "They said they need to run some more tests, so they're not letting her go home for a few of days. I promised to bring her some movies and ice cream."

Meg gave her a watery smile. "That's so sweet."

Alice rolled her eyes and let out a snort of disgust. Her sister thought being "sweet" was the highest compliment while the word had a tendency to give Alice a chill. "Don't make too much of it, sis."

Meg laughed. "Doing pro bono work, volunteering on your weekends, and now you're a candy striper? You know, one of these days people are going to start to catch on to the fact that beneath that cool-as-a-cucumber act, you're actually quite the softie."

Alice stood and set down the scraper. "Don't get too excited, Mother Theresa. The pro bono work is going to get me that promotion. I help out at the theater because *I* love to watch movies here—it's selfish motivation, really—and Ena…" She stopped as another image of a pale, lifeless-looking Ena gave her a shudder. "She's my friend."

Before Meg could get all weepy again, she added, "Plus, she has the best collection of old movies I've ever seen. How could I not be nice to her?"

Meg rolled her eyes, but she didn't argue. She knew Alice's obsession with old movies better than anyone because she shared it. It was really the only thing the sisters had in common. The shared love was their old next-door neighbor's fault. Some of Alice's earliest memories were of the nice old lady next door coming to their apartment door during her parents' fights. She'd come in, ignore her screaming parents, scoop up Alice, take Meg by the hand, and bring them back to her apartment, where she'd plop them down in front of her old TV, which was always tuned to the classic movie channel.

She'd ignore them for the rest of the time they were there, but she and Meg didn't mind. They were just happy to be out of the war zone, and those black-and-white flicks were the ultimate escape. As they got older and the next-door neighbor moved away, Meg took over the job of taking Alice into the kitchen, where their mom had an old, tiny TV set up. It was fuzzy and the audio was poor, but it got the classic movie station, and there they would perch at the kitchen counter and watch movie after movie until the fighting stopped. The fighting didn't stop after their dad left; he was just replaced by strange men who came in and out of their lives with such frequency Alice never even tried to learn their names.

Alice was the last one to leave, and she made sure to pick up the promised ice cream and movies on her way back uptown to the hospital. Hospitals always made her queasy, and on top of that, a flutter of nerves hit her as she entered the cold, sterile building, but she shoved them aside.

Odds were that she'd never see him again. That awful bit of humiliation could be buried in the past. Forgotten.

Shoulders set, she resolutely set aside her nerves and her fears and made her way to Ena's room and found her friend looking slightly less pale and far more ornery than when she'd last seen her. "Took you long enough."

"Good to see you too, Ena." She held out the bag filled with ice cream and desserts and started to set up the movie in the DVD player. Before long they'd settled in, and Ena was back to her normal cheerful but sarcastic self as she dug into her treats and they picked apart the Marilyn Monroe movie.

* * * *

Sea-green eyes and vivid red hair—they were all Nicholas could think about for the last forty-eight hours. Maybe that was why he found himself heading from the pediatric ward to the intensive care unit.

He just wanted to check up on his patient, he told himself. Well, she wasn't his patient anymore, but he still wanted to make sure she was recuperating all right. *Liar.* An inner voice that sounded suspiciously like Claudia's voice mocked him. *You're going to see if the pretty granddaughter is there visiting.*

That too.

He stopped short when he reached Ena's room. There she was, the woman he'd been fantasizing about. She'd been a wreck the other night—a sweet, adorable-looking, rumpled mess—but today, through the small glass pane of the door, he had a straight-on view, and what he saw left him breathless.

She was stunning. That flaming red hair was piled up on top of her head, exposing her long neck. Her spectacular eyes were lit with laughter and her lips…oh sweet Jesus, those lips. A perfect cupid bow, they were lush and plump and begging to be kissed. And right now they were pulled up in a smile that made his knees weak.

Holy shit. Claudia had been right. He had a thing for this girl. No, this woman. But that was ridiculous, he barely knew her. True, he'd felt an instant connection when she'd collided with him in the hallway, but as much as he believed in *the one*—love at first sight was too hard to swallow. So he'd chalked it up to lust in hindsight. True love might be too difficult to fathom, but instant desire was easy to comprehend. It had been chemistry, pure and simple.

But then he remembered the pain in her eyes when they'd filled with tears and he'd watched as she'd lost the battle to contain them. Nicholas wasn't a spiritual guy—he was a man of science—but he could have sworn there's been something more than chemistry between them in that moment. An understanding. Something at a deeper level than just physical attraction, although that had clearly been present.

Whatever had transpired between them, it was exactly what he'd been looking for. It was the singular spark that he felt when he was around Claudia and Frank and what he'd witnessed his entire life between his parents before they'd died. It was a connection.

The thought had his heart racing as he watched the beauty interact with her grandmother. What was not to like about her? She was clearly empathetic, caring, and kindhearted.

He forced himself to wait patiently, pacing the brightly lit hallway until at last he heard the movie come to an end and some movement from inside. He leaned against the wall and tried to look casual. For the first time ever he was nervous to talk to a girl. That thought made him laugh out loud. He hadn't even been nervous as a teenager asking out his first date. But there was no denying it, his palms were sweaty, and his heart was racing like he'd run a marathon.

When she finally emerged, any illusion of cool he'd tried to adopt melted away. "Hi."

She looked up, clearly startled. Her eyes widened at the sight of him, but it was impossible to tell if it was a pleasant surprise or not. "Hello," she said slowly.

Was he imaging things or was she inching toward the exit, as if getting ready to flee.

"I just came by to check on your grandmother."

"My—" For a second, her brows drew together in confusion, but then the look cleared and she once again started to back away from him. "Oh, right. Yes. How thoughtful of you."

She glanced over her shoulder at the exit, and he had the horrible feeling she was about to take off in a sprint. Her posture was tense and poised, like she was ready to run from a crazy psychopath and not the doctor who'd helped save her grandmother's life.

He shook off the fear. Maybe she was just in a hurry to get somewhere. *So then get to it, Hot Doc*, the irritating inner voice mocked. *Ask the girl out already.* He opened his mouth to do just that but then she spoke.

"I should thank you." Despite the words, her expression was closed off. All the softness and vulnerability he'd seen in her gaze the night of the emergency was gone. Her brilliant green eyes were shuttered. Her hands were filled with DVDs, the titles of which he couldn't read, but she clutched them to her chest like a shield.

"It was no problem," he said. He mentally kicked himself for the too-blasé response. Her grandmother had nearly died, and it was no problem? He tried again. "I mean, I'm a doctor, it's what I'm trained to do."

One of her eyebrows rose the tiniest fraction of an inch, but it sent a signal loud and clear. Oh shit, he'd come off like some egotistical doctor with a God-complex. He cleared his throat. "I mean—"

"Thank you," she cut in. "For everything. It meant a lot to my grandmother." As she spoke she backed away and it was impossible to ignore the fact that her tone held no gratitude, only amusement.

His dream woman was laughing at him. The thought was almost too shocking to comprehend. He found himself taking several steps toward her as she retreated. To the casual observer, it would look like he was chasing her—literally. He forced himself to stop, take a deep breath, and collect his thoughts. For the love of God, he was a grown man. A respected doctor. Hell, he'd been named on the city's most eligible bachelors list. So why the hell was he coming across like a bumbling, egocentric asshole? *Get it together, man.*

He took a deep breath. "Would you like to go out with me sometime?"

Her eyes widened, but yet again he couldn't tell if her obvious surprise was one of pleasure or horror. Whatever thoughts were going on in that pretty head of hers were locked away behind an impenetrable mask.

Her lips parted, and Nicholas realized he was holding his breath, waiting for her answer.

"No."

The word seemed to echo off the hallway tiles and through his skull. *No.* His brain refused to compute. "No? Just…no?"

She turned then and started walking toward the exit, and without realizing he was doing it, he followed her. "Are you married? Seeing someone?"

She sighed but didn't break stride.

"Look, if it's something I said…" He let his words trail off when she spun around to face him. The smile she wore was horrifyingly nice. No, not nice—pitying.

"It's not something you said. You were fantastic the other night. Really. I owe you big time."

"You owe me?" he repeated. He couldn't help it. She made it sound like she should go out with him because she was indebted to him. "You don't owe me anything. I was just doing my job. But the other night…"

He watched in confusion as she stiffened up at his mention of that night.

"The other night," he continued. "I thought maybe there was something there between us."

Her eyes flashed with something, some strong emotion that was there and gone so quickly he couldn't put a name to it. But then the shutters fell once again, and he found himself speaking to a mannequin—a stunningly gorgeous, emotionless statue. "While I appreciate your help the other night, Doctor…"

"Bale," he provided. "Nicholas Bale."

"While I appreciate your help, I'm afraid I can't go on a date with you."

He stood there speechless for quite possibly the first time in his life. This was so not going according to plan. A woman had never said no to him before. So despite the fact that some part of his brain knew he was humiliating himself by not letting this go, he couldn't stop himself from asking. "Why not?"

Her eyes flickered from him toward Ena's hospital room. "I don't live here."

Disappointment had him slumping over a bit as her words registered.

"I'm just here visiting my grandmother," she continued. Yet again she backed away from him so she was at the end of the hall. "Sorry. And thanks again."

With that, she turned and rounded the corner to walk out of the hospital... and out of his life.

* * * *

He wasn't sure how long he stood there staring after her like a giant sap. *What the hell just happened?*

It was unfair. He'd finally met someone with whom he felt *it,* and she'd run away. Worse, apparently she didn't even live in town. He kicked himself for not learning more about her. Where she lived, what she did for a living. But when the head of pediatric surgery retired from the hospital's Boston branch next year, he would be leaving the city himself—*if* he got the job. He wasn't so committed to NYC that he couldn't entertain the idea of leaving for a relationship. Or maybe doing the long-distance thing for a little while. There were ways they could make it work. Maybe if they'd had a chance to talk, to get to know one another....

He turned back to head toward the pediatrics wing when he came to Ena's door. He *had* wanted to check on his former patient, after all. And if she happened to give him some information on her granddaughter, all the better.

With a new sense of hope, he let himself into her room and watched as the old lady's eyes lit up at the sight of him.

At least someone in the family is happy to see him.

After asking about her health and her comfort, he tried to introduce the conversation as casually as possible. "I ran into your granddaughter as she was leaving."

Okay, not exactly subtle. But it worked.

"My *granddaughter?*" Ena's wrinkled face wrinkled even more as her eyes narrowed on him like he was speaking a different language. "I don't have a granddaughter."

Before he could make sense of that, her eyes widened in sudden understanding. "Oh, you mean Alice."

Alice. So that was her name.

"She's not your granddaughter?"

Ena's laugh was husky and weak. "Oh no, she's my friend. My neighbor, really. She lives in my apartment building."

Nicholas jerked back from the side of the bed as if she'd just thrown her glass of ice water in his face. And that was exactly how it felt. She lived here. In New York. And in his apartment building.

Ena was watching him closely. "You like Alice, no?"

"Hmm?" He reached toward her chart at the end of the bed in a clear-cut case of avoidance.

Her laugh said that she saw right through him. "She's single, you know."

Is she now? Now that the shock was starting to wear off, irritation took its place. She'd outright lied to him. And why? Because the idea of dating him was so horrible, apparently.

"What about you?" Ena asked point blank. "Are you single?"

Nicholas gave her the charming doctorly smile he'd perfected in medical school. "I'm not married, if that's what you mean."

She laughed and added, "Oh, I'm sure you're not at a loss for dates. Who would say no to a handsome doctor?"

She stressed the word doctor, making it sound far more impressive than a career. *Your friend Alice.* He clenched his teeth to keep the words from spilling out.

He was dimly aware that Ena was still talking about his career, telling him about how her first husband had wanted to go to medical school. Her words barely registered. All he could think about was what a fool he'd been. What a fool Alice had made him out to be.

She could have just said, "Not interested, thanks," but instead, she'd lied to him. Apparently the thought of going out on a date with him was so abhorrent that she didn't want to leave anything to chance. Better to pretend to live in another state than risk another overture from him. The longer he stood there, the more her actions ate at him.

He found himself backing away toward the door just as Alice had backed away from him. He couldn't stand here much longer simmering with anger while keeping a pleasant, detached smile firmly planted on his face.

"I'll stop by tomorrow to check on your progress," he said just as he reached the door.

Chapter 3

Nicholas sat across from Claudia a little while later in the hospital's cafeteria and watched with annoyance as she picked at her yogurt, seemingly unfazed by his news.

"You don't understand, Claud. She *lied* to me."

She glanced up. "I get it, Nicholas. Your dream woman blew you off." She shrugged before diving back into her snack. "It sucks, but it happens."

He stared at her in stunned amazement. "I never said she was my dream woman."

She rolled her eyes. "Oh please, I've been hearing you wax poetic about her unparalleled beauty and this amazing connection you felt for the past twenty-four hours. Besides, you wouldn't be this worked up if there hadn't been the spark of something real there."

He scowled across the table and folded his arms across his chest. "I guess I was wrong about that."

She finally set down the yogurt, and for the first time since he'd told her about Alice's rejection, she seemed to take his anger seriously. "Or maybe you were right," she said. Leaning over the table, her eyes were bright with mischief. "And maybe I was, too."

"Right about what?" Even he could hear how wary he sounded. But really, he knew better than anyone how stubborn his best friend could be when she got a theory in her head.

"Maybe you were right that you would 'just know' when the right woman came along," she said, with only a hint of mockery in her tone. "And maybe I was right when I said that it wouldn't be exactly how you planned."

She sat back and looked down her nose at him in that holier-than-though way she got whenever they were discussing a topic in which she had more knowledge—usually cardiology or relationships. "Plan all you want," she said, "but love never comes the way you think it will."

He opened his mouth to argue, more out of habit than the fact that he actually had an argument. But she cut him off with a wave of her hand. "I know you want simple, you want the neat, orderly kind of love affair that you think is the ideal. But love is messy. It's intense. It has its ups and downs."

Her use of the L-word had him sitting straight, temporarily frozen in disbelief. They were treading on sacred ground here—"love" was not something he threw around lightly. In fact, he'd never said it—not in the "in love" sense, at least. "Who said anything about love? I never said that I *loved* her."

"No, but what if it could be love?" Claudia shot back.

He blinked at her in surprise. What if it could be—the real deal, the happy ending, the love of his life? All the things he was looking for to complete his plans. The future, the family, the supportive wife. What if his gut was right and there really had been a connection? Didn't he have a responsibility to see it through? Or at least fight for a chance?

A nagging voice told him he'd only humiliate himself further, but that was fear talking and he shoved it aside. His parents would never have gotten together if his father hadn't chased after his mother and won her over—he'd heard that story more times than he could count. And Claudia was the first to admit that she and Frank would never have had a second date if she hadn't made it happen through sheer force of will.

"Maybe you're right," he said slowly.

Claudia's eyes lit up—most likely at the sheer rarity of hearing him admit that she was right more than anything. She leaned forward, her hands flying as she spoke, a sure sign that she was excited. "Of course I'm right. What do you have to lose, right?"

My pride. My self-respect. My manhood. He took a sip of his water and kept silent.

"This is what you wanted, isn't it?" she continued. "A connection?"

"I wanted simple," he said. But she was right again. He'd been on an endless string of dates and hadn't felt that spark he'd been looking for. Not until the other night.

Claudia ignored his comment. "I mean, the girl lives in your building, for heaven's sakes. She's practically on your doorstep. You owe it to yourself to at least *try*."

He shoved his chair back with a little too much force and was aware of several pairs of eyes turning to stare. "You're right," he said. "If nothing else, I think I'm due an explanation."

Claudia gave a quick nod. "Absolutely."

"She could have just said no if she wasn't interested. She didn't have to outright lie."

He didn't miss the fact that Claudia was stifling a laugh—one that was obviously at his expense. "What's so funny?"

She shook her head, but then a loud laugh escaped her, and she slapped a hand over her mouth to stifle it.

He raised his brows in question.

"It's just… You've never had to chase a woman before…." She looked like she might start laughing again, but she pressed her lips together and seemed to recover. "It's just so fitting that you find a woman who you feel you have a connection with and she wants nothing to do with you."

He shook his head with a scowl that was tempered with laughter. It wasn't often his friend, the revered cardiologist, lost her shit in public. It was a little funny to witness, even if she was laughing at him. "I'm so glad I can amuse you."

"I'm sorry," she said through a snort-like laugh. "I just…can't wait to tell Frank."

Standing up from the table, he moved over so he could lean down and give his friend a quick peck on the cheek. "Thanks. I owe you one."

* * * *

Maybe it was the adrenaline, but he found himself back at his Riverside apartment building a short time later, out of breath but filled with energy. He'd only moved in a few weeks before and hadn't learned all the doormen's names yet so he approached the short, balding fellow with what he hoped was an ingratiating smile.

"Hi there. I don't believe we've officially met," he said, holding out a hand toward the doorman.

He got a scowl in return and his narrowed eyes were watching him with suspicion. "I know who you are, Dr. Bale."

Nicholas nodded. "Right, right…." So he was the prick who hadn't bothered to learn his doorman's name. Point taken. "And you are?"

The scowl deepened. "Carl."

Nicholas ignored the blatant hostility that Carl was throwing his way. He would kill the man with kindness, dammit. "Good to meet you, Carl, er, officially."

Silence. Carl was certainly not making this easy.

"Look, Carl, I'm a doctor—" No, that was not the right way to go about this. Had he learned nothing from Alice's mocking response earlier when he'd tried the doctor route?

"I know that, Dr. Bale," Carl said.

Nicholas cleared his throat and tried again. "Right. Of course you do. What I meant was I helped one of the apartment buildings tenants the other night. You might have heard that the elderly woman in 11C had a heart attack the other night."

Carl gave a short nod. "Ena. Yeah, I heard. It was a crying shame."

"Indeed," he murmured, hoping he conveyed enough sympathy in his impatience to get to the point. "The thing is there was another resident there that night. She accompanied Ena and myself to the hospital. I believe her name was Alice…." He trailed off hoping that Carl might fill in a last name, but the older man's mouth was pressed together firmly.

"Anyways, I know she lives in the building, and I'd like to check up on her, make sure she's all right after being part of a traumatic event like that."

Carl's expression was hard, his face unreadable as he stared at Nicholas in silence.

Jesus, he was making this difficult. Shoving his hands into his pockets, he tried a more direct approach. "I was wondering if you could tell me which apartment is hers."

"I'm not allowed to give out apartment numbers." The response was swift and firm.

His smile didn't falter, but he bit back a muttered curse. "Yes, but I'm a doctor," he tried again, not entirely sure where he was going with this line of attack. But pulling the doctor card had been known to work in the past, and he was flailing for a way in.

Carl looked unfazed, most likely because they'd covered the doctor bit already, and stared blankly as he waited for Nicholas to continue.

"And, uh, I want to make sure she is all right, you see."

Carl's brows drew together. "Why wouldn't she be all right?"

He cleared his throat, buying time. Then he found himself repeating the same ineffective line. "She had quite a shock the other night and—"

Carl dropped the newspaper he was holding and let out a weary sigh. "Look, Doc. You seem like a nice enough guy, but you've got to understand that I'm not allowed to give out Alice's apartment number." He leaned forward as if letting Nicholas in on a secret. "You're not the first gentleman to come looking for her apartment, coming up with some excuse of why it's imperative that you see her. Christ, if I gave her apartment number out to every guy that came calling—"

"It's okay, Carl." The husky, sexy voice that came from the entryway behind him was unmistakable.

He turned slowly, knowing what he would find but needing that bit of time to mentally prepare himself for the punch in the gut that seemed to go hand in hand with seeing her.

There she was. Backlit by the front door, her auburn hair gleamed like a halo, giving her already mind-boggling beauty an unearthly air. It was her. Alice.

His Alice.

* * * *

Alice stared at the doctor who appeared to be haunting her. Or maybe stalking her.

It's okay, Carl? She'd said that for Carl's sake, to save him any more discomfort. But this man standing here in her apartment building? This was not okay. This was so far from okay.

She'd frozen at the first sight of him, disbelief leaving her as still as a statue as her brain registered what she was seeing. For a second there she'd toyed with the idea of turning tail and running. Everything in her body urged her to flee.

Shifting her eyes to the elevator, she stared straight ahead as she walked past him. She could feel the heat from his body as he joined her as if they'd planned this all along.

She didn't want to be alone with him again, but even more than that, she didn't want to cause a scene or put Carl in an uncomfortable position. This was her mess, and she would clean it up.

She waited until they were both inside the elevator before she pushed the button for her floor and turned to face him. "What are you doing here?"

His smile was slow and...beautiful. There was that word again. Not a word she would normally equate with a man, but then this wasn't any man. This was a god.

"I live here," the god said.

Oh no. No, no, no. Her stomach plummeted as she realized that not only was she neighbors with the guy who'd seen her cry, but he also knew she lived here, too. She'd known saying she was from out of town was stupid lie the moment it had slipped out of her mouth earlier at the hospital. She'd known there could be a chance that he lived in the neighborhood since he clearly worked at the hospital nearby. Somehow it never occurred to her that he might actually live in her apartment building. Surely she would have noticed him. Or she would have heard the gossip of a hot, single doctor moving in—Ena had eyes and ears everywhere, particularly when it came to single men. How had she missed this?

But that question would have to wait because they'd passed Ena's floor, which was where she was assuming he lived since that's where he'd gotten off the other day. The only stop left was her floor. She absolutely would have known if he'd moved into an apartment on her floor; she knew all of her immediate neighbors. So that must mean…

"We need to talk."

The doors opened on her floor, and there were no other residents in sight. She walked slowly toward her apartment, wariness making her procrastinate.

It wasn't that she was afraid of this guy, per se. But she was. Oh, he was no creepy stalker or crazy psycho killer—but he may have been something even worse in her eyes. He was a threat to her sanity. The fact that he'd seen through the chinks in her armor that night was bad enough, but he seemed to see everything about her. Maybe it was because of that night, but she could swear that he saw through her calm, cool act—the one she'd spent years perfecting.

He shook her foundation to its core. She knew very well how to behave around men to keep them attracted but at arm's length. She'd spent the better part of her life mastering that particular skill. But every time she saw this man, all she could think was that he'd seen her cry. And every attempt to pull up the age-old shield left her shaky and tattered—like she was fighting a losing battle.

She didn't like his effect on her, which meant she didn't like him.

Except that she did. Shooting him a sideways glance, she took in that firm jaw, the warm eyes that seemed to see everything and accept without judgment. He'd been kind to her. And to Ena, for that matter. He'd gone above and beyond….

But he was a doctor, that was his job. There was no way she would let that distract her. They reached her door, and she spun around, crossing her arms in front of her chest. "Anything you want to say you can say out here, Dr. Bale."

Hands in his pocket, Nicholas studied her from head to foot, his gaze missing nothing. Her skin came to life everywhere his eyes roamed, and she cursed her body for its traitorous response.

A wretched memory surfaced of the way she'd looked the other night—tear-stained, frumpy, and pathetic. She tried to shove the memory aside quickly. That was so not the mental image she needed if she was going to have the upper hand.

His eyes narrowed a bit. "You're blushing." It wasn't an accusation so much as a statement of fact, like "it's raining outside."

Irrational anger had her biting out the words, "I'm warm."

She didn't blush, dammit. She'd outgrown blushing ages ago, when she was a child. Her entire adult life she had never blushed or giggled or swooned. She normally would have added "or cried" to her mental repertoire of girly things she did not do…. But she could no longer boast about her stiff upper lip. Not around this guy, at least.

She thought she caught his lips twitching up at the corner as if he was suppressing a smile. Her eyes narrowed. "You wanted to talk, so talk."

"Why did you lie to me earlier?" His blue eyes held hers hostage. She found herself unable to look away.

She blurted out the first lie that came to mind. "I'm a compulsive liar."

Both sides of his mouth were twitching now, and she watched in fascination as he pressed them together in a hard line. "And here I thought you just didn't want to go out with me."

She breathed in quickly, her equilibrium once more off balance by his unexpected response. He was *laughing* at her. Which was why she didn't feel the tiniest twinge of guilt when she said, "Yeah, that too."

That wiped the laughter off his face, but her satisfaction was short-lived. He leaned in—not far enough to be invading her personal space but enough that his warm, masculine scent enveloped her, making her light-headed.

"In that case, I guess I was wrong."

She blinked up at him, temporarily dazed by his closeness. "Hmmm?" She couldn't focus on his words, not when he was this close. If she leaned in just a little she could touch him, the way she'd been dying to do since that night. If she tilted her head up and moved an inch in his direction, he would kiss her.

"I guess I was wrong," he repeated. She dimly noted that he sounded nearly as dazed as she felt. With unabashed fascination she watched his eyes darken with desire, sending her own pulse racing.

"I thought there was a connection here," he said. "A spark."

A spark. Alice couldn't stop the breathless laugh that escaped her at that understatement. This was no spark—it was electric bolts arcing, it was lightning streaking, it was a high-voltage current between them.

"I haven't been able to stop thinking about you," he said, his low voice washing over her, making her muscles weaken and tremble.

Me too. But she couldn't bring herself to say the words.

He shifted closer so he was filling her entire vision—the heat of his body enveloping her. Her senses were flooded by the sheer maleness and the primal attraction that was pulling her toward him like gravity.

"Ever since that night," he said.

He may have continued talking, but Alice could no longer hear. *That night.* The words and accompanying memory were a blast of frigid air to her overheated body and lust-addled brain. A memory, sharp and vivid, cut through the haze of desire. Her sobbing like a baby, looking like a disaster, losing her control for the first time in forever.

And he had seen it all.

The wave of horror that swept through her was made more intense by the fact that she'd nearly swooned at this man's feet. He hadn't even touched her and she'd been practically panting with desire.

Her back straightened as her muscles stiffened, arming herself physically and mentally against this man's effect. She drew in a deep breath and readied herself to reject him. Tell him that he was not welcome here—he read the signals wrong. There was no chemistry here. *Lie, lie, lie.*

Before the words could come out, he leaned over, closing the distance between them and claiming her lips in a kiss that was tender and gentle.

The initial contact robbed her brain of all thoughts—her protests dying in her throat as pleasure rippled through her. His lips moved against hers, gentle but insistent. There was no hesitation as he urged her lips apart, his tongue seeking, relentless until she parted for him, allowing him to take full possession, his hand cupping the back of her neck, tilting her head for more access. The force of his desire made her moan, and the sound seemed to snap his control.

His free hand, which had been setting lightly against her hip, moved around her waist and he pulled her up against him with an urgency that left her breathless. She was pressed against him from head to toe, his chest a solid wall against her breasts, and the hard length of him pressed against her lower belly, making her ache between her thighs.

A hunger swept through her, leaving her mindless and needy as her hands tried to touch him everywhere, her lips matching his intensity, and her tongue meeting his thrust for thrust.

He pulled back first, leaning his forehead against hers as they struggled to catch their breath. Her hands itched to pull him back in for more, but she held herself still, willing her body to stop aching.

This was wrong. Hadn't she decided to turn him away? This man was dangerous. He'd seen her vulnerable, he saw through her bravado. She needed to keep him away.

But her body was not having it. Even as she told herself to reject him, her fingers buried themselves in the short hair at the back on his neck, and she found herself rubbing up against him, her breasts crushing against his chest as her belly rubbed against his erection.

His groan was low and pained. "We shouldn't," he said, his voice barely more than a growl.

No, they shouldn't. That was her line. But if she pushed him away now, her body would never forgive her. She would lie awake all night tossing and turning, imagining what might have been.

Screw that. Since when did she run away from a hot sexual encounter? She never had before, so why the hell would she do it now. To deny herself would be to give this man more power than he was worth. This was physical attraction, that was all. He'd all but said it himself. She could do attraction—lust and desire were nothing to fear. That was one of the reasons she kept her love life to three-date maximums. Just enough time to explore the physical attraction without getting attached. Why would it be any different with this man?

It wouldn't, not as long as she set the ground rules. Excitement added to her breathless anticipation. She could do this—she could explore the chemistry here between them on her terms.

A wicked, delicious idea was forming, and before she could think it through—before her rational mind could talk her out of it—her body made the decision for her. "One night," she whispered, her hands moving from his neck to his shoulders and down over his hard chest.

He drew back slightly, his gaze fixed on her. "What?" The mindless, drugged expression was gratifying—at least she wasn't the only one reeling.

She didn't bother to repeat what she'd said. It didn't matter if he was on board, what mattered was that she knew the rules. One night. Not three like the others—three would be too dangerous. But one…one night would be enough to get him out of her system, enough to satisfy her curiosity and quench this overwhelming desire.

And then he would be gone. For good. Just like the others.

She watched as the dazed look in his eyes was replaced by regret. "I'm sorry. I shouldn't have done that," he started. "I didn't mean—"

She cut him off with a kiss—rising up on her tiptoes to press her lips against his, sucking on his lower lip until he caved with a groan. His arms around her tightened and he moved one hand down to her lower back, pressing her against him. When she arched her hips in a silent invitation, his mouth on hers turned brutal and he slid his hand down further to cup her ass and bring her hips up to meet his.

The hard length of him rocked against her core, and the exquisite torture of it had her head falling back with a moan. He dipped his head to kiss her neck and nibble on her ear.

As she lost her balance, they stumbled back a couple of steps until her back hit her door with a dull thud.

Oh Jesus, they were still in the hallway.

She turned and fumbled with the key that was in the door, her breath coming in gasps as he came up close behind her so her bottom was cupped against him, his arms tightening around her waist, his hands slipping over her stomach and up her waist.

The door burst open just as his hands were about to cup her breasts.

"Inside," she gasped, stumbling through the doorway. "Now."

* * * *

He should leave. This was getting out of hand. He wanted to date this woman, not take advantage of her. Three dates, that was the rule, right? Three dates and then sex. Not sex and then dates. But he could tell himself that until he was blue in the face and it wouldn't have made a difference. An army of men couldn't have torn him away from her at that moment.

As soon as they were both inside, she spun around so she was back in his arms, and he did the unthinkable—he grabbed her and lifted her up into his arms like a goddamned caveman. But rather than protest, she wrapped her long legs around his waist and grinded up against him.

Holy shit, she was hot. This drop-dead beautiful redhead was a ball of flames in his arms. Every time sense attempted to rear its ugly head, she would silence it with a wicked stroke of her tongue or a tempting touch of her hands until finally he forgot why he was fighting it.

She pulled back, her fingers turning to the buttons of his shirt. He glanced around the spacious studio until his eyes fell on the bed. In three quick strides, he brought them to the edge of the bed, and he gently laid her down.

Holy hell, she was gorgeous. Those green eyes were heavy-lidded and hypnotic, her lush lips parted, waiting for his next kiss. She was dressed for business, with a silky red top and a tight-fitting pencil skirt that hugged her hips and showed off her hourglass figure. Wiggling up onto her elbows, her lips curved up into a seductive smile. "Are you just going to stand there all night or are you going to undress me?"

Words escaped him. It was like his best fantasies had come to life. Then he snapped into action, his body taking control while his brain took a leave of absence. He fell on top of her, bracing his weight on his elbows as their bodies pressed together, meshing and molding—the perfect fit, even through the layers of clothes. Her head fell back, her eyes closed.

She felt it, too —this connection.

Whatever doubts and reservations he'd been battling fell away, crushed by the blind lust that coursed through him. He saw the same desire reflected in her heavy-lidded gaze and it drove him crazy, adding fuel to the fire inside him that erased all thoughts and had his lips moving over the sensitive skin at her neck, needing to taste her, to feel her. Needing to be as close to her as humanly possible—desperate to become one with her.

Her head arched back, giving his mouth full access to the sweet, tender skin below her ear and her pants for air went straight to his head. He wanted this to be good for her. Better than good, he had to show her how right they were together.

Her arms wrapped around him, kneading his shoulders and neck as she pulled him closer until her breasts were pressed against his chest, making them both moan.

His fingers made quick work of her blouse and she'd already undone his buttons so soon they were topless and pressed together, the feel of her lush curves against his hot skin almost more than he could bear. He pulled away long enough to look down at her, soak in the beauty that lay before him. "God, you're gorgeous," he groaned.

She pulled him back to her and he thought he heard her say, "No talking," before her lips claimed his again, luring him into a deep, long kiss that erased all words from his vocabulary.

His hands came up to cup her breasts and her whimper against his lips made him ache with desire, yes, but also an innate protectiveness. She was his to cherish. His to protect.

His to adore.

He dropped his head to worship her perfect breasts, covering them with kisses before finally caving in to his desire and settling his lips over a nipple, sucking gently as she moaned and writhed beneath him. Her hands in his hair held him to her as he licked and kissed one nipple before moving on to give equal attention to the other.

"More," she whispered above him, tugging him up to meet her lips once more for a hot, messy, open-mouthed kiss that echoed the primal need coursing through him.

Her hips were wriggling beneath his, arching up trying to get closer. With every move, he hardened further until he was mindless with red-hot desire. In unspoken communication, she lifted her hips, and he unfastened her skirt, tugging it down, and tossing it aside.

She was clad in nothing but pink silk panties, and he fought the urge to tear them off her and claim her in one quick thrust.

He had to make this good. He needed to be sure she wanted this—wanted him. Coming to lie beside her, he slipped a hand over her panties, biting back a groan of pure male pleasure of the feel of her hot wetness as she spread her legs for him and pressed herself against his palm, her head tossing from side to side.

She was ready. She needed this as badly as he did. He moved over her, leaning down to place one light kiss to the V between her thighs, his lips brushing over the pink silk softly, briefly.

She cried out his name at the feather-light touch and Nicholas lost his battle for composure. Tugging off the last barrier between them, he cast her panties to the side. "Condoms?"

She threw a hand toward her nightstand. "Top drawer."

He found the box, wrapped himself in a condom, and settled in between the thighs that parted for him in welcome.

When he buried himself inside her, he lost himself completely to the overwhelming and entirely new sensation of coming home. She was the perfect fit, and as her liquid heat surrounded him, he heard her moan against his throat. She felt it, too. This coming together—it was perfection.

He moved slowly inside her, wanting to draw out the delicious torture, needing to take her to the farthest heights before they found their release.

Her hips met his thrust for thrust, and he watched in fascination as her head fell back, her eyelids fell shut, and she surrendered herself to him. It was as humbling as it was erotic.

His forehead fell against hers as the tension grew and the pace intensified—only when she cried out in ecstasy did he allow himself to follow her over the edge.

After they came back to earth, he lay prone at her side as their breathing evened. He'd followed her over the edge, he thought again. And he would do it again in a heartbeat. As he started to drift off, it struck him.

He would follow her anywhere.

Chapter 4

Nicholas woke to the sound of a dresser door slamming shut. He blinked in the dim light of the bedroom as his brain raced to make sense of where he was.

Alice's bed, in her apartment. A grin spread across his face at the memory of the night before.

Alice came out of a walk-in closet, fully dressed with her hair up and makeup done. Nicholas forgot how to breathe. *Stunning.* "Morning, beautiful."

She didn't look in his direction as she headed toward a vanity and began sorting through a jewelry case. When she spoke, her voice was cold as ice. "You need to get going."

Nicholas stared at her back, certain he'd heard wrong. "Excuse me?"

He heard her sigh before she spun around to face him, her face set in a mask of indifference, her eyes hard and unreadable—the exact opposite of the vision he'd seen in bed hours before after their third round of lovemaking, each more incredible than the last.

"I said, 'You need to leave.'" She drew the words out like he was a dimwitted moron. "I have to get to work, and I can't leave with a stranger in my apartment."

"A stranger," he echoed. He found himself staring at her, his eyes scrunched up in confusion—as if, if he stared at her hard enough he could make sense of what she was saying. "You want me to leave?"

Even to his own ears, he sounded…pathetic. Still, her eye roll was straight up rude.

"Did I do something?" he started. Irrational fear was rapidly replacing his confusion. They'd had fun the night before—hadn't they? But maybe he'd moved too quickly. She'd seemed into it, but maybe he should have given her more time. He'd rushed thing like an idiot and now—

"You didn't do anything," she said, turning back to the mirror to put on her earrings. Her voice was flat, expressionless. "We had a good time. Now it's over."

He saw her shrug. "Time to move on."

"So you—uh—" He couldn't think of anything to say. His mind was a blank. Granted he hadn't thought this far ahead last night, but he hadn't expected this. He'd assumed they would talk this morning. He'd been looking forward to waking up with her in his arms. Before falling asleep he'd envisioned a morning of getting to know each other—talking and sharing. Maybe making plans for a proper date. "You don't want to… do this again?"

He cringed as soon as the words left his mouth. Shit. She probably thought he was just using her for sex. "I didn't mean—"

Her laugh cut him off. It was short and harsh and completely lacking in humor. "Nice try, stud, but I think three times was enough for me. Besides, I don't have time for a quickie."

Right. No time. She reached down and tossed his pants onto the bed, and he automatically reached for them even as his sluggish brain tried to process what was going on. "I didn't mean did you want to do *this* again," he said eloquently as he waved his hand toward the bed. "I meant—"

She turned back to face him, impatience written all over her as she crossed her arms and waited for him to continue. He had to get this right. He had to fix whatever he'd done to mess this up.

"I meant," he started again. "I'd like to see you again." He finished putting his pants on as he stood beside the bed, and took a step closer to her. She didn't back away but he saw her stiffen.

"I'd like to take you out, if I may." He took another step, slowly, carefully. A part of him worried she might bolt if he spooked her.

She raised one brow, the cold cynicism in her gaze rooting him to the spot. "What, like a *date*?" It was the sneer that accompanied the word that flooded his blood with ice water.

"Yeah, something like that," he said. "Not exactly unheard of, especially not after…" Yet again, he filled the space with a gesture toward the bed.

She laughed again. "Sex. The word you're looking for is sex." Now it was her turn to take a step toward him, her eyes fixed on his. "We had sex. It happens. Now it's over."

"But I thought…" The words were out before he could stop them. Everything about this was wrong. His stomach churned as his heart picked up its pace.

Her lips curled up in a smirk as she tilted her head to the side. "You thought…what? What did you think?"

He paused for a second, knowing how poorly this would go, but he couldn't stop himself. "I thought we had a connection."

She froze, her eyes trained on him. And then her head fell back and she laughed. "A *connection*?" she said, cold laughter filling her voice and hardening her eyes once more. "That's cute."

For the first time that morning, the confusion fell to the side to be replaced with anger. She was laughing at him. After he'd told her he thought there was something between them. After they'd *slept* together. "So you won't even consider going on a date with me."

She stopped laughing then, but the look in her eyes was dangerously close to pity. "No offense, Doc, but I don't date." She looked him up and down. "Especially not men like you."

They were standing several feet apart, but he could have sworn she'd slapped him across the face. His head jerked back at the harsh words. "What is that supposed to mean?"

She sighed again as if he was a tiresome child. "Look, you're not my type, that's all. So…can you see yourself out, or shall I show you the way?"

* * * *

Two days had passed, but he couldn't stop thinking about Alice—about that night and then that morning. It had been night and day—literally and figuratively. And no matter how much he thought about it—how many times he replayed it all in his head—he couldn't make sense of it.

Maybe that was why he was standing in Ena's doorway, shuffling uncomfortably as he debated whether to enter or walk away. He hadn't even talked to Claudia about the other night—mainly because he wasn't sure what to say. But he needed to talk to someone. And who better than someone she knew and trusted.

"Are you going to stand out there in the hallway, or are you coming in?" Ena's voice carried through the door, and he found himself laughing at the old woman's no-bullshit ways. Letting himself into the room, he found her propped up in bed, a game of solitaire spread across her lap.

"So," she asked, looking up with a knowing glint in her eyes. "Are you here to play cards with me some more, or were you hoping to run into my gorgeous young friend?"

He fell into the seat beside her. "Maybe a little of both?"

He was rewarded with a grin as she swiped up the cards and began to shuffle. "You play rummy?"

Glancing at the clock, he said, "I've got time for one game before my next meeting."

She started to deal the cards. "So what happened between you two? Are you the reason she's only calling these days, making excuses to stay away from the hospital?"

He didn't try to hide his surprise. "She's avoiding the hospital?"

Ena gave a short nod. "Oh, she's been sending me treats and gifts—she's a sweetheart deep down, you know."

His mind flashed on a memory of her cold, hard glare as she kicked him out of her apartment. *No, he didn't know.*

"But," Ena continued, "she's been awfully squirrely about why she can't come visit in person. And we were supposed to watch *Singin' in the Rain* last night, one of her favorites."

Nicholas wasn't sure how he was supposed to respond to that, so he muttered something about being sorry, although he wasn't sure why.

She was waiting for him to speak, clearly hoping he'd have the answer. "I, uh, I think perhaps there was a misunderstanding between us," he said.

Her eyes narrowed on him. "A misunderstanding, huh?"

Before he could reply she let out a loud sigh. "Don't tell me, she's pushing you away."

Nicholas wasn't sure he'd heard her right. "What do you mean?"

Ena shook her head. "Never mind. So what is it you want from me?"

He could appreciate that she was a straight shooter and he tried to match her in her honesty. "I was hoping you could explain why she acted the way she did—"

She was shaking her head before he could even finish. "No can do. Sorry, kid, but Alice is one riddle you'll have to figure out on your own." Her watery brown eyes met his. "But I can promise you, she's worth the effort."

His shoulders slumped, his traitorous brain flashing on her brilliant smile, the wicked, mischievous glint in her eyes that spoke of intelligence and a sharp wit, the husky seductive voice. *Are you going to stand there all night, or are you going to undress me?* "Yeah, I have a feeling you might be right."

After they'd played in silence for a little while, each apparently lost in thought and not speaking much, Ena finally piped up. "I'll tell you what. I can't get in the middle, but I can give you her phone number."

His chin shot up and his gaze locked on hers as a burst of something dangerously close to hope had his blood pumping. "I'll take it."

The moment she gave him her number, he dialed and cursed under his breath as he was sent straight to voicemail. With a glance up at Ena, he typed out a text. Nothing complicated, just a reminder that he was there and he wasn't going away.

Any chance you've changed your mind about that date?

He set the phone down by the edge of Ena's bed as they continued the game, but he noticed that Ena's eyes flickered to the phone to see if there was a response almost as often as his did. By the time the game was over, the atmosphere in the room had grown mellow, sad almost.

His phone was deathly silent.

* * * *

Alice couldn't take her eyes off the screen. *Any chance you've changed your mind about that date?*

Nope. She hadn't. She definitely had not changed her mind. But hearing from Nicholas had not been part of the plan and his phone call, followed by his text, set her on edge. He should have gotten the hint and disappeared by now. But no, for some reason the sexy doctor was still in her life—unseen, perhaps, but he hadn't gone away. The worst part was, she didn't know what kind of game he was playing. She'd slept with him and then treated him like dirt. Either he was a glutton for punishment or he had an ulterior motive—no sane man would still be trying to woo her, for God's sake.

"Waiting for an important phone call?" Meg asked.

Alice jumped on her barstool. Her sister had been waiting on some stragglers from the late lunch crowd and now was standing right next to her, watching her watch her phone.

Meg laughed at her start of surprise. "What has you so jittery?"

Alice shook her head. "Nothing. My boss just asked to see me in his office this afternoon, but I have no clue what it's about."

That wasn't entirely untrue—Dixon did ask to see her—but that wasn't why she'd been staring at her phone.

Meg nodded slowly. "Mmm-hmm." Her tone was filled with disbelief. "That doesn't explain why you've been acting so weird these past couple of days."

Alice's stared at her sister. "What do you mean?" Her confusion was genuine. Sure, she'd been feeling a bit off since her night with the doctor, but she'd thought she'd been doing a damn fine job of covering it up. She'd met with Tamara and the others just the night before to finalize some plans for the theater's fundraiser and she'd been totally on her game.

Meg was eyeing her with suspicion, but she let it drop.

Alice let out the breath she'd been holding. Thank God. The last thing she needed was to have to lie to her sister, who always seemed to see right through her bullshit no matter how cleverly she hid the truth.

And the truth was that she was miserable. No, not miserable. She was... dead inside. That was it. She stirred the ice in her club soda as Meg waddled behind the bar to cash out one of the remaining customers. Dead inside. Maybe that was a tad melodramatic. But it was the only way she could describe the sensation, even to herself.

She'd done the right thing when she'd kicked Nicholas out of her apartment. She knew that. Yes, there had been some guilt at the sight of the hurt look in his eyes. She'd been cruel—but she'd had to be, she reminded herself. Clean breaks were the only real breaks.

Still, that knowledge hadn't made the hollow, empty pit in her chest any easier to bear. It was entirely illogical. She didn't know the guy well enough to be attached. Still, this frozen feeling wouldn't ebb. Normally if she was this down she'd go watch a Fred and Ginger movie with Ena, but her friend was still in the hospital and that place was currently off-limits.

There was no way she would risk running into the sexy doctor again—not when she was feeling so...off, like her world had slipped off its axis. She didn't trust herself to be around him.

But this would pass. It was just hormones or a vitamin deficiency or something. Soon enough she'd get back on the horse, so to speak, and that one-night aberration would be a thing of the past.

The only problem was—she glanced down at her phone again, aware that Meg was still watching her like a hawk. He was supposed to hate her after the way she'd treated him. She'd been horrible. Mean and cold. Why the hell was he reaching out to her?

Why was he being *nice*?

It didn't make sense. That feeling of the world being off kilter kicked in again, leaving her dizzy.

"You don't look so good. Are you sure you're all right?" Meg leaned over the bar, her big belly bumping up against the row of liquor bottles beneath it with a loud clinking sound.

"I'm fine," Alice said with a sigh. "You're the one who's nine months pregnant. I should be asking you that. Do you need to sit?"

Meg rolled her eyes. "You barely let me lift a glass during the lunch rush. I think I can handle closing out a few tabs."

At that reminder, Alice tore off the waitress apron she'd wrapped around her slacks to keep her office clothes clean. "I like helping out on my lunch break."

Meg raised a brow in disbelief, but she didn't argue. "Between you covering my lunch shifts and Jake hovering over me every time I attempt to clean up around here—I'm starting to feel useless."

"Then maybe you should do as we keep telling you and go home and get some rest."

Meg scowled, but whatever argument she was about to give was cut off by Tamara's arrival. The petite blonde had clearly run over from the theater next door because she was winded, her cheeks flushed. "You will never guess what just happened."

Before they could even try to guess, Tamara hurried on. "The developer who's been talking to the owner about buying the place? He took the deal off the table. He found another location."

Alice couldn't stop the squeal of excitement. It was girly and high-pitched, but it was also well-deserved. The whole crew had been terrified ever since they'd found out that Ben's company had approached the owner to buy.

"Did Ben call off the deal?" Meg asked. Her voice was breathless, and Alice knew why. Tamara did too, judging by her answering grimace. "I have no idea. I hope so...."

They were all rooting for Ben to finally stop being a spineless ass and realize that he was in love with their friend. Finding out that his company had been the one to potentially destroy their theater had been a crushing blow for Caitlyn, who was entirely too sweet and trusting for her own good. But if Ben had finally come to his senses... Maybe he'd called off the deal for her.

The ice inside her chest almost thawed at the thought. Alice liked Ben, she had from the first time Caitlyn had brought him by to hang out with the crew at Cagney's, Jake and Maggie's bar. He was funny, charming... And she saw something in him that she could relate to. Maybe it was his cynicism or his tendency to keep the people he loved at arm's length—either way, she thought the two of them could be friends one day. If he would ever get his head out of his ass and realize that Caitlyn was the best thing that ever happened to him.

"I hope Ben did this for Caitlyn," Tamara said as she plopped down onto the stool, her eyes practically glowing with excitement.

"Me, too," Meg said with a sigh. "But even if he didn't. This is amazing news. The Ellen still has a chance to find a buyer who actually appreciates its history."

The alarm on Alice's phone interrupted their celebration. "Sorry, kids, I've got to get back to work. Can't be late for the boss-man meeting."

Tamara gave her a hug good-bye but when Meg leaned in to peck her cheek, she whispered, "Whenever you want to talk about what's really bothering you, you know where to find me."

Alice backed away with a quick wave, ignoring the flicker of pain. She didn't want to talk. Not now, not ever. She was more than happy to be the sounding board for her friends' man troubles and life dramas, but that was so not her. She'd made that decision ages ago.

She did not do drama. Nor did she do relationships, or pining, or crushes, or any other stupid romance nonsense. That was all meant for the movies, thank you very much.

With that thought, she hopped in a cab back to her office in Midtown. When she arrived, she paused in the lobby to take a look in the floor-to-ceiling mirror. Smoothing back the hair that had fallen out of its chignon during the lunch rush, she applied one coat of lipstick for good measure before getting on the elevator.

She hadn't been lying about being a little nervous about this meeting. The hope that this might be the day that she finally got her promotion had her stomach flip-flopping with excitement. Placing a hand over her stomach, she ordered it to remain calm. *Do not get ahead of yourself.*

The only thing worse than disappointment was getting one's hopes up and having them crash down around you. That much she knew to be true. How often had she watched her mother fall madly in love, over-the-moon ecstatic about whatever loser had come along this time? And every single time it ended the same way—heartbreak and despair. Their mother a broken, crying wreck, losing herself in a bottle of vodka rather than playing with her kids.

She may not have been much of a mother, but at least she'd taught Alice one valuable lesson: never get your hopes up. It only ended in tears. And tears she would not do.

Her mind flashed back to that awful night at the hospital, and she shuddered at the memory of Nicholas's tender gaze as he held her tight.

That could never happen again. To lose control like that... It would never happen again.

The floors ticked by one by one, giving her another minute to calm her nerves and straighten her back. The trick behind being confident, cool, and utterly under control? Fake it 'til you make it. She'd learned that one on her own.

By the time the elevator doors parted, Alice was herself once more. She pretended not to notice the stares of her male coworkers as she strode past, chin tilted up, eyes focused on the boss's office door.

This was it, the promotion she'd been waiting for. Somehow not even that thought could ease the hollow feeling. *You should be happy.* Her heels clicked against the tiles. *You've earned this.*

Dixon's door was shut, so she knocked once before entering. He looked up with a wide smile. As a long-time veteran in the marketing and public relations industry, he was quick to smile and always had a compliment handy.

With salt-and-pepper hair and a perma-tan, despite the weather, his smile revealed shockingly white teeth. Alice thought he would make an excellent salesman if he ever decided to switch careers. As it was, he half stood as she entered—a nod to his age that he still thought men should stand when a lady entered a room.

"Alice! Gorgeous as ever," he said, gesturing toward the seat across from him.

She returned his smile and settled into the seat, folding her hands in her lap to keep from fidgeting. *This was it.*

"How's your theater event going?" His eyes crinkled at the corners, as if he was struggling not to smile even as they sat there discussing business.

"Fine—great," she amended. "Everything is falling into place."

He was still watching her, waiting for more.

"The theater got some good news, actually," she said. "We just found out that it's no longer in imminent danger of being sold to a developer who wanted to tear it down."

"That's great," he said, though she had the feeling he couldn't care less about the little downtown theater.

"Still," she hurried on. "The fundraiser will be key to raising the funds we need to get the theater back to its original glory and hopefully find a buyer who shares the same goal."

He was nodding, but his eyes had a slightly dazed quality. Yeah, he had so not called her in here to hear about The Ellen. Impatience had her squirming in her seat. *Get on with it already!*

"Mr. Jamison was very impressed to hear that you volunteered to lead a charity event," he said.

Mr. Jamison! He was Dixon's boss's boss. The head boss. The biggest of the bosses. For the first time she let herself experience a flicker of hope. *This was it. Here it comes….*

"So impressed," Dixon continued, "that he has handpicked you to lead an event that is near and dear to his heart."

Alice blinked in surprise. No mention of a promotion, but this was big, this was huge, this was—

"It's another pro bono event for charity."

This was bullshit. She struggled to keep her smile in place. Another charity event? So she could spend more time and energy working for free? No, thank you.

Dixon turned to a stack of files on his desk and handed one to her. "It's for the new children's clinic at Hudson Hospital."

Alice silently cursed like a sailor, but her smile never faltered. Hudson Hospital—where Ena had been rushed for her heart attack. Where Nicholas worked. That place was haunting her.

"As you may know, Mr. Jamison and his wife are heavily involved as donors at the hospital."

Alice nodded, though this was news to her. She'd met the head honcho once at a Christmas party, and all he'd talked about was golf.

Dixon leaned over the desk and his eyes locked on hers. Oh no! She knew this look. She'd seen him do this to clients. He was in full-blown sales mode. "Mr. Jamison asked for the best to lead this project, and once I told him about your recent work and the way you've spearheaded the fundraiser at the theater—well, he was impressed, I'll tell you that."

Despite herself, a flicker of hope fought its way through her irritation. Impressed, huh? That sounded good. She risked being bold—after all, she hadn't gotten where she was by being meek. "Impressed enough to promote me to senior associate?"

Dixon's eyes widened and his mouth fell open, but a split second later his head fell back and he roared with laughter. Face red from laughing so hard, he jabbed a finger in her direction. "I like you, kid. You remind me of me when I was your age."

Alice grinned. "I'll take that as a compliment."

"You should!" He sobered a bit as he studied her. "And to answer your question—yes. If you make a success of this event, I guarantee you that Mr. Jamison will reward you with the promotion. But don't tell him I told you so."

She gave him a wink. "It's our little secret."

He chuckled at her saucy tone. "So, you'll do it?"

Alice leaned over to snag the folder from the top of his desk and sighed. It wasn't the ideal scenario, but it was better than nothing. One more pro bono event—a few more weeks of working her butt off for free—and the promotion would be hers. She could hold out a little longer. "I'll do it."

Dixon clapped his hands together. "Fantastic. Mr. Jamison will be glad to hear it."

She made a move to stand up but he held out a hand to stop her. "Wait right there, my next meeting is with the contact from the hospital who'll be leading this from their end. He should be here any second."

Alice's jaw dropped at her boss's audacity. "You planned this? You knew I would say yes?"

A knock at his office door had him standing and walking around the desk to answer it. As he passed her he patted her shoulder. "I told you, kid, you remind me of me. Of course you'd take the gig."

She didn't have a chance to respond before he swung open the office door for the hospital's contact.

Alice's heart sprang into her throat before dropping to the pit of her stomach. *Noooo.* This could not be happening.

Wearing a blue button-up shirt and a pair of khakis, Nicholas stood in the doorway looking like a J. Crew model come to life. He was smiling at Dixon, but then his gaze turned from her boss to Alice, and she watched in horrified fascination as he froze, his face a mask of confusion.

"Dr. Bale, so glad you could make it," Dixon said, extending his hand for a handshake.

She could practically see Nicholas's brain working, clicking the pieces into place as Dixon introduced her as the lead on the project. "I'd like you to meet Alice Klein, a rising star in the PR world."

Alice recovered from the shock first. She had to take control, make sure that Nicholas didn't ruin this for her.

"Dr. Bale," she said, hand extended and a bright smile plastered on her face. "Pleasure to meet you."

His eyes widened for a moment, but then he took her hand in his and gave a peremptory shake. "Ms. Klein," he murmured.

His voice made her insides quake, but externally she never faltered. She kept a look of polite attention on her face as Dixon gave her background and explained more details of the project. When he was done, he clapped his hands together. "Well, I'm sure the two of you want to delve right in to business. I'll, uh…" He backed away toward the door. "I'll just leave you to it."

He disappeared through the door, and Alice heard the door close behind him, but she didn't watch him leave. She hadn't been able to tear her gaze away from Nicholas. His blue eyes were locked on hers, but the emotions there were unreadable.

The door clicked shut and the ensuing silence was deafening.

Alice's brain scrambled to come up with something to say—something to make this right. But holy freaking Christ, this was a disaster. This was her big chance to prove herself to the big boss—she couldn't walk away from it.

His gaze softened on her. Tender, sweet. Shit. There was no way she could work with this man. She couldn't be around him—it was bad enough they lived in the same apartment building, but at least there she wouldn't be forced to spend time with him.

He broke the tense silence first. "Hello again." His low voice rumbled through her, resonating in her chest and making her heart ache inexplicably.

Shit, shit, shit. Panic added an edge to her voice. "What are you doing here?"

He smiled at her, his head cocked to the side as if trying to read something in her face and body language. As if trying to understand her. To get her. *Good luck, buddy.*

"I thought your boss made that pretty clear," he said, a hint of laughter in his voice. "I'm spearheading the new children's clinic. This fundraiser is *my* project."

Right. She knew that. Still, his calm rattled her, adding fuel to the chaotic emotions that had been lying dormant since their encounter the other night. Now they were back with a vengeance, and so many hit her at once, she couldn't sort through them. All she knew was that a knot of anxiety had lodged in her chest and made her feel like she was choking. Panic had adrenaline coursing through her veins.

"Did you know about this?" Her voice was shrill, and his head jerked back in surprise.

"What?"

"Did you know that I worked here? Did you ask for me?" The words were coming out as accusations even though a voice in the back of her head was insistently trying to remind her that he'd looked just as shocked as she'd felt when he'd first walked through the door.

"No," he said. "God, no. I didn't even know your last name, let alone where you work."

He was telling the truth—of course he was. This man had never been anything but decent and honest with her. But that didn't seem to make a difference to her rattled emotions. She was standing on shaky ground, and she needed to get out—she needed to run.

He took a step toward her and she inched back, nearly tripping over the chair behind her. His gaze was too intense, too all-seeing…and way too kind. She didn't deserve kindness, not after the way she'd pushed him away. What was wrong with this guy?

He took another step toward her so he was only inches away, close enough that she could feel his heat and smell his masculine scent. It made her dizzy, confused. He was close enough that he could reach out and touch her. If that happened she would be well and truly lost.

Alice acted on instinct. Moving quickly, she stepped around him, dodging his arm that reached out to touch her. "Alice…"

Whatever he was going to say, she couldn't hear it. "I've got to get out of here."

"Alice, wait."

But she didn't pause, didn't stop to think…didn't even try to make an excuse for her sudden retreat. It wasn't until she reached the crowded sidewalk that she could catch her breath or even comprehend what she'd done.

Holy shit, she'd run away—from her office, from Nicholas…and from the career break she'd been dreaming about.

What the hell had she done?

* * * *

Alone in the office, Nicholas didn't know if he should punch a wall or run after her. *What the hell was that?*

He should leave. He shouldn't stay here when her boss would come back undoubtedly curious as to why his star employee had bolted out of here. But instead, he stared at the empty office before him dumbfounded, his brain too muddled to take action. In the past sixty seconds he'd gone from shocked to confused to angered to…. Well, he didn't know what he was feeling now.

He should be pissed. She was the one who kicked him out and now she had the audacity to make it sound like he was following her. Like he'd set this whole thing up.

And he might have been angry…if he hadn't seen it there in her eyes, plain as day. *Terror.* It had been there and gone so quickly he might not have noticed it if he wasn't so obsessed with those remarkable sea-green eyes. But as it was, he'd been mesmerized once again and hadn't been able to look away—and so he'd caught it.

So instead of being pissed that the woman who'd slept with him, rejected him, and ignored him had thrown wild accusations his way before running away… He found himself feeling sorry for her.

Pathetic, possibly, but there it was. His heart ached for the girl. No, the woman. She'd been all woman the other night, but here in this office when surprise and confusion had toppled her carefully maintained image, he'd seen a glimpse of Alice as a little girl, scared, cornered, and lashing out in defense.

But why? That was the question.

Before he could contemplate it any longer, Dixon came in looking entirely too happy. But once he saw that Nicholas was alone in his office, his face fell. "Where is Alice?"

Nicholas stared blankly for a moment but then hurried to make up a lie. "She was called away suddenly—a family emergency, I believe." When Dixon's forehead furrowed, he quickly added, "But she and I have made plans to meet up later to discuss the upcoming fundraiser."

That cleared the concern from the older man's expression, and his broad grin was once again in place. "Wonderful, wonderful. Trust me, Dr. Bale, you are in excellent hands with our Ms. Klein here. She is responsible, reliable, and committed." He patted Nicholas's back as he led him out of the office and toward the elevators. "Yes, sir. Alice is relentless—she'll be by your side throughout all of this, you can count on that."

* * * *

A little while later Nicholas found himself recounting the entire scene to Claudia. She'd texted to see if he wanted to meet for drinks, as he was heading back uptown. His shift was done for the day and he wasn't on call... Why not? Maybe Claudia could shed some light on Alice's strange behavior.

"So…you're still working on the event with her?" Claudia's nose was crinkled up in disbelief, her glass of wine halfway to her lips where she'd apparently forgotten about it as his story had gone from bad to worse. He'd had to catch her up on the events of the other night—well, the safe-for-friends'-ears version at least, followed by the morning after from hell, and finally the afternoon's latest turn of events.

He shrugged. "I assume so. I mean I can't step aside from this clinic. You know that. If this clinic opens, I'll be the surefire pick to head up the pediatrics department at the Boston hospital."

She nodded in understanding—she was well aware of his career goals and their timeliness—his next logical step was to be the chief pediatric surgeon, and opening the clinic had been his chance to show the board that he was a capable leader—it helped him stand out above the rest of his competition. But if the whole project was a dismal failure because he couldn't get along with the PR company who'd offered to sponsor the main fundraiser—well, he could kiss the promotion good-bye, no doubt.

"Maybe she'll quit," she said.

He frowned. "Maybe. But you're missing the point."

Claudia finally sipped her wine and set it down. "And that is?"

"I don't want her to quit. This could be the perfect chance to get to know her better. I mean think about it. We would be on the same team—we'd have a common goal, we'd—"

She held a hand up. "Easy, Casanova. I get it. This would be your chance to woo her."

He took a long swig of his own beer. When she put it that way it sounded ridiculous.

Leaning over the table, she pursed her lips as she studied him. "Are you sure this girl is worth it?"

Before he could reply, she continued on. "I mean you've been saying all this time that you want something simple. Something *easy*."

He winced to hear his own words thrown back in his face. Because that was what he'd wanted. Until...until... "That was before I met Alice."

Claudia cringed a bit as she patted his hand. "Sorry, Nicholas. I hate to say I told you so, but..."

He rolled his eyes. "You love to say I told you so. And I'll admit it. You were right—I finally found someone who I might possibly have feelings for, and it is definitely not going according to plan." *That might be the understatement of the century.* He studied his beer as if the rising bubbles might provide some answers.

He heard Claudia shifting uncomfortably across from him and knew her well enough to know that she was struggling to say something he wouldn't want to hear.

"Spit it out, Claud."

He looked up to see her frowning at him. "I'm just wondering if maybe... I mean, have you thought of the possibility that you might want this woman so badly because... Well, because you can't have her?"

He blinked at Claudia as he processed the words. His initial response was to get annoyed and tell her, "of course not," but he was a doctor, a scientist—he was fully capable of objectively looking at the situation, and her theory made sense. He had never truly faced rejection from a woman before. It wasn't ego talking, it was the simple truth. He was handsome, successful, and never suffered from any major personality defects that would make him abhorrent to the opposite sex.

"Maybe," he said slowly. But then his memory called up an image of their tryst together—the way she'd looked up at him in the hallway. She'd given herself to him—hell, she'd practically seduced him—and that hadn't ebbed any of his attraction or the connected feeling he'd experienced every time he looked into her eyes. If anything, it strengthened it, knowing that the intense attraction was shared.

He set down his beer. "Maybe, but I don't think so."

Claudia was studying him, but she nodded quietly at his admission.

He toyed with a coaster on the table. "But I'd like the chance to find out either way. I mean I've made it well into my thirties, and this is the first time I've felt this way. I owe it to myself to at least try to see this through, don't I?"

Claudia's smile was slow and filled with a motherly pride. "Yes, you definitely do. And I think it's brave of you to face rejection, all in the name of love—"

"Uh-uh, I didn't say love," he interjected.

She ignored him. "So what are you going to do now?"

He inhaled deeply as he thought it over and let the air out in a sigh. "I guess I have to find my runaway coordinator."

* * * *

That was easier said than done. He tried knocking on her apartment door five different times throughout the evening but if she was home, she wasn't answering. He tried texting and calling—but it was like shouting into a void. She'd gone underground.

His last hope was lying in a hospital bed. He showed up, flowers in hand, the next day during a break in his rounds.

"Doctor Handsome," she called out when she spotted him. "Aren't you a sight for sore eyes? I'm starting to think they're never going to let me out of this place."

"It's for your own good," he said. "I'm sure your doctor just wants to make sure you're a hundred percent before sending you home."

She waved off the comment with a "yeah, yeah" that told him he was saying what she'd already heard a hundred times before.

Smiling up at him, she asked, "To what do I owe the pleasure?"

"I wanted to see how my favorite card player is doing." She was laughing as he walked in, giving him a knowing smile.

"What did she do this time? Don't tell me she's still avoiding your calls."

He shoved his hands in his pockets. "Worse I'm afraid. She ran away from me." After he recounted the incident at Alice's office the day before, Ena let out a low whistle. "Oh boy, that girl has got it bad."

He blinked. "Excuse me?"

Shaking her head, she laughed softly. "I can't tell you how to make things right with our prickly little friend, but I can tell you this—I know exactly where she'll be tonight if you still want to try."

Chapter 5

Alice stood on the sidelines, trying to revel in her success despite the fact that the hollow, frozen pit in her chest had been replaced by a burning misery. She'd take that numbness over this pain any day of the week.

With a forced smile, she took in the crowd around her in their period-piece costumes. The invitations to the gala had made it clear that guests were to dress up as an old movie star or their favorite classic character, and some of them had gone above and beyond.

The theater looked perfect, the attendance phenomenal—she'd even spotted the legendary playboy billionaire Gregory Blanchard wandering around looking like a matinee idol in an old-school tux. This party was officially a success.

Even shy Tamara, looking eerily like Veronica Lake, seemed to be having a great time, with her roommate Marc at her side. She'd lost sight of Caitlyn, but she'd seemed to be holding up pretty well when they'd talked earlier, considering the fact that she was nursing a broken heart. Maybe this party was exactly what her friend needed.

Yes, because this party was doing such a stellar job of keeping you distracted. You've only replayed the wretched incident at the office, what—a thousand times since you've arrived?

She shoved aside the caustic inner commentary. That was different. She wasn't nursing a heartbreak, but dealing with a professional nightmare. Of course she couldn't just brush that aside.

Her face ached from smiling. Only a few more hours and she could get out of there, put on her comfy pajamas, and curl up in front of a good old movie.

She bit the inside of her cheek to keep a groan in as she smiled and waved to Meg and Jake, who were passing by on the other side of the lobby.

What had she done? The panicky voice she'd been trying to silence all day came back with a vengeance. She saw Meg still eyeing her, concern written all over her face, and she forced her smile up a notch. *All is well.*

Nothing to see here. It's not like I just threw away the opportunity of my dreams in a moment of insanity.

Maybe she could still salvage this situation. If she could talk to Dixon, make him see that she would be better suited to another project...that was near and dear to Mr. Jamison's heart. Yeah, because those came along every other day.

Maybe she could convince Nicholas to step away from the project. He was a busy doctor doing busy doctor things. Surely he didn't care all that much about a fundraiser...even if it was for children in need...and even if he was a pediatric surgeon.

Dammit, why did everything about him have to be so...so...*nice.* It was hard to dislike a guy who spent his days saving kids' lives. But then add the fact that he not only accepted her horribly rude behavior, but still pursued her anyway.... Who did that? And then he'd smiled at her at the office, like he'd actually been happy to see her.

"What's wrong with you?"

She turned to find Meg at her elbow, hovering beside her.

"Nothing. Why?"

Her older sister knew her too well. Meg's eyes were narrowed in on her. "I'm worried about you. You've been acting weird lately."

Alice sighed a little too loudly, judging by the looks they got from a passing couple dressed as Clark Gable and Carol Lombard. "I'm fine."

"You've been saying that for days now, and I don't believe you. What's up?"

She looked at her sister. "You're the one we should be worried about. Haven't you had that baby yet? What has it been, eleven months? Get that thing out of there already."

Meg ignored her teasing. Really, her sister's sense of humor had been less and less forgiving the bigger she'd gotten these last few months—particularly when it came to her size.

"I won't be distracted—you've been avoiding talking about what's bothering you for too long." Meg crossed her arms over her chest. "Spill it."

For a moment, she considered telling Meg everything. *Well you see there this guy, and he's amazing... And he saw me cry!* Yeah, no. Meg would never understand. Though they'd grown up in the same broken, toxic home, as they'd grown older it had become rapidly apparent that the sisters had wildly different takeaways from the experience.

Meg had gone off to college desperate to find the kind of stability and home life she'd never had growing up. And she'd succeeded almost instantly when she'd met Jake her freshman year of college, and had surrounded herself with her close-knit group of friends like Caitlyn, Tamara, and Marc.

And now, with the baby on the way, she had it all—the family she deserved. The stability and normalcy she'd always craved.

But Alice had learned a different lesson way back when. She'd left their broken home knowing that she would never make her mother's mistakes. There was no way she'd do what she'd done—fall for every guy she met, make herself vulnerable, and hang it all out there, just waiting to get her heart stomped on. What had that done for her mother? Left her crushed and broken and unable to take care of her daughters. That was not the life for Alice. She had a career, friends, and a family in Meg, Jake, and her soon-to-be-born niece. She didn't need a man and she sure as hell didn't need love.

So Nicholas had gotten past her defenses somehow. She could salvage this situation because, when it came down to it, she was strong and she knew what she wanted. *The promotion.*

Meg was still watching her with so much concern that it flooded Alice with guilt. Shit, she hadn't meant to make her sister worry. So rather than delve into the whole story, she said, "It's a work thing."

Meg's eyes narrowed in a look she knew well—she was trying to figure out if she was telling the truth. Well, she was. Just not the whole thing.

"You didn't get the promotion that you wanted?" she asked.

Alice tilted her chin up. "Not yet." But she would—Nicholas be damned. She was smart and savvy, and she deserved this. For the first time all night some of the tension eased out of her. Yes, she'd made a mess of things in the office, but it wasn't too late to fix this.

She would take on the hospital event and prove herself to Mr. Jamison and there was no way in hell she'd let some guy get in the way of that.

Meg was looking past her toward the door. "Do you know that guy?"

Alice turned and froze, her breath rushing out of her lungs. Nicholas was standing just inside the doorway, scanning the crowd. Dressed in his hospital scrubs, he looked ridiculously out of place…*and hot.* A good foot taller than those around him, he looked like an Adonis come down to reign over mortal men.

She shook her head at the fantasy. *Stupid, Alice. Nicholas is here, and he's obviously looking for you—deal with it.*

But her feet refused to move, and she found herself staring, lips parted for much-needed air. Something had her frozen in place. *Fear*, a voice whispered. No, that wasn't it. Of course it wasn't. It was just that he had an effect of her, which was…unusual.

"Are you okay?" Meg asked. "Do you know that doctor?"

Meg's familiar voice was the dose of reality she needed to break the spell.

What had she just been telling herself? That she could deal with this man. He would not get in the way of her success. This was a test—he was a test—but she'd never failed before, and she sure as hell wouldn't fail this time.

She took a deep breath and gave Meg a reassuring smile. "Fine. Just fine. I'll go deal with this guy."

Nicholas spotted her as she was walking toward him, her face set in a grim expression. So why the hell did his eyes light up? And why was he grinning at her like that...like he was happy to see her?

Maybe the man was an idiot—a glutton for punishment. Doctor or not, he clearly wasn't in his right mind.

"How did you find me?" It was hard to keep her voice cold and her expression severe when he was giving her that charming smile—like she was the best thing he'd ever seen and not some nasty shrew who'd kicked him out of her apartment and then run away from her own office like a lunatic.

"Ena told me I might be able to find you here," he said.

Ena. Alice's hands clenched at her sides at her friend's betrayal. No, not betrayal—Ena probably thought she was doing her a favor by sending the hunky doc her way. She never could get it through her stubborn head that she wasn't looking for love...or a husband—the two things Ena seemed to think made the world go round.

"That doesn't explain why you're here," she said.

His smile never faded despite her less than enthusiastic reception. She wasn't even entirely sure he'd heard her. He seemed to be too distracted by her outfit to respond. His eyes moved over her body, taking in her auburn hair, which she'd styled in waves around her shoulders, and the form-fitting black satin strapless dress and long black gloves. The way his eyes darkened as they touched on every curve had her traitorous memory flashing back to their night together—to the way his hands have moved over her, relentless and tender at the same time.

"Are you an old movie buff, or is this part of the job?"

His words brought her back to the present, but she ignored the question. There was no way she was going to chit chat with this man about her very passionate—and very private—love of old movies. "What are you doing here?" she asked again.

He took a step toward her and she had to force herself to stand still and not back away. Or worse, run away. Again.

His voice was so low she nearly couldn't hear him over the crowd talking around them. "I thought we should talk about what happened yesterday."

She pressed her lips together in annoyance as a stubborn childish voice protested. *Why did they have to talk about it?* She didn't want to deal with him or work or anything else.

But that was immature, and worse, it would do nothing to rectify the situation at work. Hadn't she just convinced herself that she needed to deal with this situation so she didn't throw her promotion opportunity out the window?

She drew in a deep breath. This was her chance. Now was the time.

Taking him by the arm, she steered him toward the theater's entrance. She didn't need her sister or one of her curious friends coming over to meet the hot stranger when they were in the middle of talking business. And she'd spotted enough curious looks from Meg to know it was only a matter of time before she pounced.

He followed her lead, and it wasn't until they were out in the cold night air, that he stopped and turned to face her with a look of amusement. "Embarrassed to be seen with me?"

Crossing her arms over her chest, she drew in a deep breath to start talking, but was distracted by the sudden change in his expression. Gone was the amusement, and in its place was something darker…hotter. His eyes were fixed on her breasts and she looked down to see that her arm-cross move combined with her strapless gown had her breasts nearly spilling over, giving him an eyeful.

She dropped her arms and his gaze shot back up to her face, his face flushed—though whether from embarrassment at having been caught or from desire, she couldn't tell. Telltale heat crept into her own cheeks at her lapse in poise. Dammit, she did not blush. Or at least she hadn't until this guy came along.

Straightening her shoulders, she told herself to shake it off. So she seemed to have a tendency to humiliate herself in front of this man—so what? He would soon be out of her life for good.

"I'm glad you're here," she started. She was about to finish with "I've been meaning to talk to you about the fundraiser," but before she could get the words out, she saw his lips twitch with barely concealed amusement.

"Really? You have a funny way of showing it."

He was right, of course. She'd been a bitch—not just when he showed up at the party but more often than not since the moment they'd met. Come to think of it, when she wasn't being a bitch, she was being a basket case or throwing herself at him like some sex-crazed fiend. So why was he being so nice? And why did he keep calling her, and smiling at her, and—

"You were saying," he prompted. Was it her imagination, or was he struggling not to laugh. At her. *No one* laughed at her. Well, no one who wasn't her sister or a close friend.

She cleared her throat and started again. "I'm glad you're here. We need to talk about how we're going to handle this fundraiser situation."

He outright laughed then, his blue eyes lit up with amusement as he gazed down at her. "Situation?" He drew the word out, making it sound ridiculous.

"Yes," she said through gritted teeth. "Obviously we can't work together—"

"Why not?" Some of the amusement had faded, but his new intensity was no better.

She opened her mouth to respond but couldn't summon up the words. Why not? *Because you make me uncomfortable. Because you were supposed to be a one-night stand. Because you saw me cry!*

But she couldn't admit to any of that, so she stood there mute, trying to think of a good reason. She saw the concern in his eyes, and it made her stiffen. He took a step toward her, reaching out a hand to touch her arm. "I'd like to work with *you* on this fundraiser," he said, his voice so soft and gentle it nearly brought tears to her eyes. God, what was it with this man and his direct effect on her tear ducts?

And every other part of her body. The light touch of his hand on her arm had her stomach muscles tightening, partly with the need to run away but with something else, too. Blood rushed to her head, clouding her mind, and heat pooled low in her belly, making her ache. She was acutely aware of his nearness, as if his body was emitting a gravitational pull. How was it possible that she was getting turned on by the most harmless touch imaginable?

Jerking her arm away from his hand she took a quick step back and was relieved when he stayed where he was, giving her space.

"Look, Nicholas, I'm sure you're a nice guy and all but I don't mix business with pleasure." There. That sounded good. Logical, even. "This fundraiser is important to me. Very important. Perhaps there's someone else at the hospital I could work with—"

"It's important to me, too," he cut in. "Not only am I passionate about the clinic and its mission, but it's crucial for the next step in my career." He ran a hand through his perfect hair. "I've worked my ass off to get where I am at the hospital, but I need to get this clinic off the ground if I'm going to prove I can lead a unit of my own."

Somehow that blindsided her. While she knew he was a doctor, obviously, it hadn't occurred to her that he—or anyone, really—could be as career-driven as she was. She tended to assume that it all came so much easier to other people. It always seemed to from where she was standing.

"Me, too," she blurted out and then instantly regretted the admission. She did not need this man knowing any more about her life. But he was watching her, waiting for her to explain her stupid remark so she hurriedly added, "I mean this is a big opportunity for me to prove that I deserve a promotion."

He studied her for a moment, his expression unreadable. "Well then, why don't we just work together?"

Her stomach fell. No! That was not the answer. She managed to keep silent, but he must have read the horror in her eyes because he quickly added, "We're both adults. And professionals. I think we can manage to put aside whatever awkwardness might be between us to get the job done."

He tilted his head down so he was a little closer to eye level. "Don't you think?"

What the hell was she supposed to say to that? *No, I don't think I can be mature enough to work with you. I can't look at you without remembering what you looked like naked.* That memory was enough to make her pant for air as lust took control of her body and mind.

Shit. If he could get over it so easily, so could she. Right?

They were both distracted by the sound of someone running toward them. Only when the runner reached the glowing lights of the theater's marquee did she recognize who it was. *Ben.*

Her heart squeezed with joy on Caitlyn's behalf. There was only one reason Ben could be here—he'd finally realized what an asshole he'd been and was here to win her back. Thank God. Caitlyn deserved her happily ever after. And so did Ben.

Despite everything he'd put her friend through, she'd always liked Ben. Maybe because he reminded her of herself. The first time she'd met him at Cagney's, she'd spotted it—the way he kept a distance between himself and Caitlyn. The way he sought out fun and adventure but steered clear of commitment. She could definitely relate.

But look at him now. A flicker of pity shot through her. He was leaning against the theater panting, like he'd just run miles to get here. The poor schmuck had gone and done it—he'd gone and fallen in love.

Another one bites the dust.

Ben's eyes moved from her in her gown to Nicholas in his scrubs, studying them. She waited for him to take a crack at Nicholas, but he turned to her, more than a little wariness in his eyes.

"Hey there, sailor," she said.

Surprise flickered in his eyes—no doubt he'd expected her to chew him out for the shitty way he'd broken her friend's heart. And he was right to think that, especially since she'd vowed physical harm if he ever hurt her. But there was something so pathetic about him just then that she didn't have the heart to pile on more pain.

The surprise passed and his eyes focused on her, taking in the dress, the hair, the gloves. "Gilda?"

Alice nodded, barely suppressing her amusement as she watched him eyeing the front door, looking like a man possessed. The poor fool knew Caitlyn was in there and the pitiful puppy dog look on his face was almost more than she could bear.

"What are you waiting for? Go on and win back your girl."

In a second, Ben had disappeared into the lobby.

Alone once again, Alice faced Nicholas, her confidence slightly shaken by the sight of Ben, though she couldn't say way. Maybe because he was a loner like her…and he'd crumbled. Not that she wasn't happy for Caitlyn, but still. It was a loss for Team Anti-Love, for sure.

She pulled herself up to her full height, which, even with heels, had her looking up at him. Her forehead just reached that ridiculously square jaw of his. She cleared her throat. "So it's agreed then," she said, feeling the need to spell it out. "We'll work together on this project, but it will be strictly professional."

He didn't answer immediately, and her stomach clenched with irrational fear.

When he finally spoke, it came out slowly, as if he was carefully choosing each word. "I like you, Alice." He paused and she felt his gaze studying her reaction. If that was the case, he probably hadn't missed the fact that she'd held her breath at those words.

Don't panic, she told herself even as the panicky sensation stole over her. They were just words. Harmless words. It wasn't like he was proclaiming his love for her. Besides, he barely knew her. Once he got to know her he'd change his mind—they always did.

As if reading her thoughts, he continued on in that same slow, gentle tone, as if he was afraid of spooking her. "I don't know you very well. But I'd like to change that. I think working together could be a great way to fix that."

She forced herself to release the breath she'd been holding as naturally as possible. "I wasn't aware that was an issue we needed to remedy," she said as lightly as she could manage.

His flicker of a frown showed her that her barb had struck exactly as intended. *Be as sweet as you want, Prince Charming, I'm not falling for it.*

Instead of backing away as he should have, he took a step closer so they were nearly touching. She tried not to hold her breath, but his deliciously male scent was making her dizzy and the feel of his warm body so close made her mouth go dry.

He reached out and lightly touched her chin so she was forced to meet his gaze.

"I like you," he said again in that slow, deliberate way. "But I won't push you."

Her scattered brain clung to the second part of that sentence. He wouldn't push her. And while she had no reason to trust this guy—every instinct told her he meant what he said. He was far too old-fashioned and gallant to lie about that.

Gallant. The word nearly made her laugh aloud. She couldn't remember ever thinking anyone was gallant—that was a word reserved for fairy tales and princes. She supposed it was perfectly fitting for the knight in shining armor before her as well.

"Fine," she said, taking a step back and stumbling a bit as her heel met with the side of the theater's brick wall. She glared at him in warning when he reached out to steady her, and he drew his hand back quickly.

She inwardly cursed at her clumsiness at such a crucial moment. Why was it she lost all sense of grace and composure when this guy was around? Wetting her lips she tried again, this time sticking out a hand for him to shake. "Fine," she said. "It's agreed. We will work together, but we will keep it strictly business."

His lips parted as if to protest, but she saw him concede with a small, self-deprecating laugh. He reached to take her outstretched hand, and she instantly knew she'd made a mistake. His hand was warm and enveloped hers, sending electric energy pulsing through her.

A handshake—such a simple touch, but so intimate.

She shook her head in disgust as she tugged her hand out of his. There was nothing intimate about it. It was a business deal.

So why were her hands shaking as she looked up into his warm gaze? And why was he looking at her like she'd just agreed to more—like this was something more. He leaned in then and for one heart-stopping moment she thought he was going to kiss her. And the worst part was that she wanted him to. A little part of her nearly closed the distance between them, impatient to feel his lips on hers even though her brain was screaming, "Bad idea!"

But just before their lips met, he moved his head slightly to the side so his lips were next to her ear. "We can agree that this is strictly professional," he said in a low voice that made her shiver. "But you can't stop me from liking you."

Alice gasped and her mouth fell open as she tried to think of the appropriate dismissive comment. The snide sarcastic remark that would turn him off. But her brain was a blank, and all too soon he turned around and walked away from her, leaving her stunned and shaken.

Chapter 6

An hour later, Alice was bundled up in her comfiest pajamas, an open box of Oreos in front of her sitting next to a glass of milk. Sophisticated it was not, but she'd needed comfort, not class. Besides, no one was here to judge her.

Even as she thought it, her door buzzer rang, startling her off the couch. Who the hell…? Nicholas. He knew where she lived, maybe he hadn't been content with the way they'd left things. Her heart hammered in her chest, but for the life of her Alice couldn't figure out if it was due to nervous excitement or terrified dread.

She still didn't know when she swung the door open, but her heart stopped its hectic pace at the sight of her sister in her doorway, her lips pinched tight.

"Meg! What's wrong? Is everything okay?"

Meg held up a hand to silence her as her all-seeing gaze took in Alice's boxy pajamas and the black-and-white flickering in the dark apartment. "You're here?" she said, her voice shrill. With a sound of disgust she whipped out her phone to text someone.

"What are you doing?" Alice asked.

"Telling Jake I found you and he can call off the search and rescue team."

Alice's stomach plummeted. Guilt gnawed at her. She probably should have told someone at the party before she'd taken off like that. But she'd been…rattled. No, rattled didn't cover it.

You can't stop me from liking you. His words had echoed through her and she'd found herself standing there alone with a confusing mix of emotions. She'd been inexplicably pleased, she couldn't deny it. Something about the certainty in his voice—the sincerity—filled her chest with a joy that even now threatened to burst out when she wasn't paying attention.

But terror had far outweighed the happiness. So much so that she wasn't sure how long she'd stood there, paralyzed outside the front doors of the theater, shaking from the cold and…something else. It wasn't until a tipsy couple stumbled out of the theater and bumped into her that she was finally spurred into action.

And she couldn't bring herself to go back to the party—she just couldn't. Not to make idle chit-chat or catch concerned glances from her sister and friend, and certainly not to watch Ben and Caitlyn have their happily ever after. She just couldn't. So she'd run.

But now, watching Meg finish up texting and put her phone away with a weary sigh, Alice was consumed with guilt. Opening the door farther to invite her sister in, she mumbled, "Sorry, sis."

Meg rolled her eyes as she stormed past her and fell onto Alice's white leather couch. "It's okay. I needed to get out of there and off my feet anyways." With that she propped her feet up on Alice's coffee table. She shot her one more scowl. "But you shouldn't have worried me like that."

Alice fell onto the couch beside her. "I know."

And that was it. Meg had a quick temper but never held a grudge. "So what happened?" she asked, reaching for a cookie.

Alice feigned nonchalance, even though she knew she couldn't fool her sister. "Nothing. I just got tired."

Meg snorted. "Right. Miss Party Planner Extraordinaire suddenly developed an aversion to parties?"

Alice picked up a cookie and toyed with it as she considered how much to tell her sister. "It's a work thing." That wasn't a total lie—this situation with Nicholas did have to do with work. She took a bite of the cookie, pleased that she'd told the truth, albeit a partial truth.

"Uh-huh," Meg said, her eyes never wavering from Alice. "So it had nothing to do with the hot doctor you were talking to?"

Alice sighed. "We're working together. That's all."

"Is it?" Meg asked. "Because I'm pretty sure I saw some sparks flying. And Ben said you two looked…intimate."

Alice gaped at her sister. "Ben said that? Since when did Ben become an expert on *intimacy?*" She drew the word out mockingly.

Meg grinned. "Since he got his head of out his ass and told Caitlyn he loves her."

Alice gasped. She couldn't help it—her heart had clenched painfully, but it was the good kind of pain. The joyful kind. Her friend deserved to be happy, they both did. "Thank God," she said on an exhale.

Meg nodded. "Right? About time."

Alice laughed at her sister's disgruntled tone. Meg had no patience when it came to her friends finding their soul mates. What she never seemed to understand was that, A, not everyone wanted to find a soul mate and, B, not everyone who did was lucky enough to meet said soul mate during their freshman year of college like she had.

"What happened? What did he say?" Alice asked.

"Uh-uh, you are not distracting me with talk of Caitlyn and Ben," Meg said, her arms folded over her chest in a stubborn pose Alice knew all too well.

She widened her eyes in her best innocent look. "I don't know what you mean."

Meg sighed. "You're trying to distract me, and it's not going to work. You had me worried tonight and I'm not leaving here until I know why you fled like that."

When Alice failed to respond, Meg patted her belly. "You made me stressed. The least you can do is spill."

Alice fell back against the couch cushions in defeat. There was no way she was going to outlast her stubborn sister; she might as well tell her the truth. "I, uh…"

Meg was waiting expectantly but Alice found herself at a loss for words. She *would* tell the truth…if she knew what it was.

"Oh my God," Meg murmured beside her.

Alice turned quickly to face her. "What?"

Her sister shook her head. "This is worse than I thought. You like this guy."

Alice jerked back so quickly she nearly toppled over on the sofa. "What? No. No, I don't."

Meg's mouth slammed shut, but she continued to stare with those all-seeing eyes and that smug look.

"I don't like him," Alice snapped. "I barely know the guy."

Meg's silence was irritating and grating on her nerves. It was like she was outright saying, *Yeah, right.*

"I slept with him, okay?"

Meg didn't so much as blink. But then, Alice wasn't exactly known for being chaste.

"And I didn't expect to have to work with him." She bit the inside of her lip to shut herself up, but Meg's expectant silence was all but begging to be answered. "Okay, fine, I never expected to see him again. Oh, maybe every once in a while since he lives in this building, but that…that I could handle."

She stared at the TV screen, barely registering the movie that was playing as she replayed that evening's run in for the millionth time.

"But working with him—that you don't think you can handle?" Meg's quiet voice cut into her memories.

"What? Oh…no. I mean, yes, I can. Of course, I can. I'm a professional."
Even to her own ears, she sounded like she was protesting too much.
Dammit, he wasn't even around and he had her rattled.

When she turned to face her sister, she caught her small smile that she
was struggling to hide.

"What are you laughing at?" she demanded.

Meg shook her head. "Nothing, it's just—I've never seen you so…"

"So, what?"

Meg shrugged. "Out of control, I guess. You always seem to have it all
together. You're always so…"

Cold. Hard. Poised. Confident. These were all words she'd heard used to
describe the vibe she exuded. It was a façade she'd worked hard to create—
an illusion years in the making. And he seemed to knock it down without
even trying the moment he entered a room or her thoughts, for that matter.

Meg never finished her sentence, turning to her with a wide grin instead.
"I like this guy."

Alice gaped at her. "You haven't even met him."

Meg shrugged. "I don't have to. I can see the effect he has on you right
in front of my eyes. Maybe he's exactly what you need."

Alice shook her head as her sister was talking. Oh no. No, no, no. She
caught the excited glimmer in her sister's eyes. It was her crazed romantic
look—the one that screamed matrimony and motherhood. Meg had never
gotten it through her thick skull that the monogamous life was not for her.
She'd thought her sister had finally given up, but watching her obvious
excitement now, it was clear she was still as obsessed as ever.

"Don't go there, Meg. I'm serious. I don't want to hear your theories
about true love and all that crap."

Meg pressed her lips together in a dramatic show that she would keep
her romantic thoughts to herself.

Alice rolled her eyes at her sister's response, but she was stifling a laugh.
"Okay, fine. Say what you have to say."

Meg shook her head. "No, you don't want to hear it, and I can respect that."

Her sister sounded like she had much more to say on the topic. "But?"

"But," Meg continued on quickly. "I do think it's rather…telling…that
you reacted the way you did tonight."

Alice tried to muster up a defensive response but was temporarily stuck.
Her reaction *had* been over the top. Running away like that? Letting his
words get into her head? She'd overreacted in a major way.

She shook her head quickly. That was it. Her sister was right, her reaction
was out of proportion, and that was inexcusable. He may rattle her, but she

was in control of her responses. She would dictate how she acted around him and how their relationship did—or did not—progress.

She straightened her shoulders at the thought. Control was practically her middle name. She'd been leading boys around on a string since she was old enough to know what boys were. This man would be no different. She'd been thrown off by the sudden shifts in his place in her life that was all—in the course of a week he'd gone from nameless savior, to hot lover, to annoyingly persistent rejected lover, to business partner. It was enough to make anyone's head spin.

But not anymore. She'd just needed some distance. Some perspective. Both of which she had now, thank you very much. She turned back to her sister with a satisfied smile.

"Dr. Nicholas Bale is my temporary colleague, but that is all."

Meg raised one brow as she peered at her over her glass of milk. "Are you sure about that?"

She nodded with more confidence than she felt. "Absolutely. I'll make sure of it. I'll make sure we stay focused on the business at hand, and once the fundraiser is over, we'll go our own ways."

* * * *

Nicholas held his phone to his ear to his shoulder as he carried two steaming hot cups of coffee into Alice's office building. There was every chance that at least one of these cups of coffee would soon be spilled all over him, but it was a chance he was willing to take. Coffee wasn't much of a present to soften the blow, but it wasn't like he could walk into Alice's office with roses and chocolates—not if he expected to live.

"Are you sure this is a good idea?" Claudia asked on the other end of the line.

No. "Yes."

"I mean it's almost like you're blackmailing her into a date—"

"It is *not* blackmail," he interrupted. "I'm just…upping the ante a bit. Besides, she really does need to meet the hospital's biggest donors, and what better way than to do it than at tonight's gala?"

"As your date," Claudia finished in a dry voice.

"As my colleague who is accompanying me," he corrected. He ignored the uneasy feeling in his stomach that may or may not have been guilt, thanks to his friend's less-than-supportive response to this latest plan.

But really, what other option did he have? Alice had taken the "business only" aspect of their relationship to the extreme. If he called, she sent him to voicemail and followed up with an impersonal email—usually one laden with bullet points. If he stopped into the office, he would inevitably find that she had stepped out or was conveniently in the middle of a meeting. The last time he'd tried to surprise her with a visit, one of the assistants had informed him none-too-politely that he should really consider making an appointment ahead of time to avoid wasting his time.

He'd *tried* to make an appointment, he'd wanted to tell her, but Alice either canceled or rescheduled every time.

But it wasn't like he could fault her work or call her unprofessional. In the week and a half that had passed since their run-in at the party, she had been incredibly industrious, coming up with a variety of gala themes, venue suggestions, and entertainment options. She didn't seem to need his help with any of it, but she dutifully kept him in the loop—the cold, unemotional, business-only loop.

Well, not anymore.

"She can't avoid me forever," he told his friend, whose stifled laughter he pointedly ignored. "Look, I've got to run. I'm at her office building. I'll see you at the gala tonight."

"I wouldn't miss it for the world," Claudia said, her voice filled with laughter. "And tell your reluctant date that I can't wait to meet her."

He hung up on her without saying good-bye. It was clear his best friend thought he was nuts—and maybe he was because he sure as hell couldn't explain his behavior. This was exactly what he didn't want. He'd never wanted complicated or difficult—this wasn't the way it was supposed to be. But try as he might to convince himself of that, he couldn't shake this obsession. He'd never found himself thinking about any woman the way he did Alice. She haunted him when he was awake and in his dreams.

He opened the front door and strode through the glass-walled lobby of her office building with quick, determined steps. If his parents' marriage had taught him anything, it was that a real connection was worth fighting for. He couldn't say for certain if this was love or just an infatuation—all he knew was that it was a first for him in so many ways. The first time something hadn't come easily, for one. The first time he'd veered off plan—not that in pursuing Alice he'd ditched his life plan or anything, career-wise, he was still right on track—but blatantly throwing himself at a woman who claimed to have no interest was definitely not how he'd imaged his personal life unfolding. He was supposed to have met a nice, sweet, amiable woman by now. One who liked him in return and who welcomed his advances.

He shook his head in self-disgust as he waited for the elevator. Instead, he'd gone and fallen for the one hot, single woman who had zero interest in dating him.

But he couldn't help who he felt the connection with. It wasn't like he'd set out to fall for her. Not that he'd fallen, he corrected himself quickly. It was much too early to tell if she was the one.

That was why he needed more time with her. He glanced down at the coffees in his hand as the elevator dinged and the doors slid open. That was exactly why he was here, coffee in hand in lieu of an olive branch as he set out to strong-arm his crush into going on a date with him.

He shook his head in mild disbelief at his own predicament before striding down the hall toward the offices. The assistant closest to Alice's office came out from behind her desk quickly when she saw him. "I'm afraid Alice is in a meeting at the moment."

Right. Of course she was. He flashed the young girl his most charming smile. "That's quite all right. I'm actually here to see Mr. Dixon and Mr. Jamison today."

She blinked at him a few times, her jaw slack as she seemed to be digesting this bit of news. He moved to continue down the hall but turned back quickly to see the assistant still watching him.

"If you see Alice, would you please be so kind as to tell her about our meeting? Something tells me she might like to join."

She nodded mutely, her mouth still slightly agape. He turned then and headed toward the largest office at the end of the hall.

Now it was just a matter of waiting. Something told him he wouldn't be waiting long.

* * * *

Alice's head snapped up as Rosie burst into her office, panting for air. "Rosie? What is it?"

Breathlessly the assistant related her story, and before she could finish, Alice was on her feet, heading toward the office door, an anxious pit roiling in her stomach. "Meeting with Dixon and Jamison? Did he say why?"

Rosie shook her head as she followed her into the hallway. The assistant kept talking but Alice tuned her out, her brain was sorting through the possibilities. *He was there to complain about her work.* No, she'd been doing her work just fine. So maybe she hadn't been terribly inclusive with her teammate on this one, but she'd been doing all the work. He couldn't possibly be here to complain.

Her internal pep talk did nothing to assuage the rising panic. By the time she reached the door and swung it open, her stomach was churning. *What the hell was he doing here?*

All three men turned to her with a bright smile as the door slammed against the far wall with far too much force. She winced inwardly at the

Maggie Dallen

sound, but her sudden and dramatic entrance didn't seem to faze the others in the room.

"Alice," Dixon said in his typically jovial tone. "So glad you could make it."

Mr. Jamison turned to her with a less ecstatic smile but a smile nonetheless. "Yes, Ms. Klein, we're so happy to hear how much progress you've made with the children's clinic fundraiser."

Alice tried not to lose her cool in the face of praise coming from the big boss—the boss who hadn't known her from Adam up until…well, now. "Thank you, sir. It's been—"

"Dr. Bale has been singing your praises," he continued, beaming at her as he patted Nicholas's arm. She risked a quick glance at Nicholas. *Had he?*

He, like the others, seemed happy as could be. Too happy. Suspiciously happy, considering she'd been avoiding him like the plague since that night in front of the theater. Her eyes narrowed slightly in suspicion and his eyes darted away from hers, back to the others.

She may not know him well, but that quick, evasive look spoke volumes. She just knew that Dr. Nicholas Bale wasn't one to avoid eye contact—not unless he had something to hide.

What was she missing here?

It didn't take long to find out.

"Nicholas here was just telling us about how the two of you will be attending tonight's gala to meet the donors and spread the word about our new clinic," Dixon said.

All eyes were on her, and she did her best to keep her cool. Steeling her features into a smile, she murmured, "Did he now?"

That set Jamison off on a little tirade about what a wonderful idea it was that they network together and how beneficial this would be for her. Just think of all of the connections she'd make.

Alice nodded and smiled, but she was only half listening. All of her attention was focused on the man standing beside her, ignoring her stares. Anger had heat spreading throughout her limbs and up to her cheeks.

She would kill him. Yup, she was definitely going to kill him.

But she forced a brilliant smile when Dixon and Jamison turned her way. "Well, you kids have to get ready for the big night. Alice, why don't you take off a little early today?"

"Great idea," she said through clenched teeth.

Through a haze of blind fury she followed Nicholas out of the office, remembering to grab her purse and jacket from the office before following him down the hall to the elevator. She remained silent as they waited for the doors to open.

It wasn't until they were in the elevator and the doors had clicked shut that she spoke. "I cannot believe you," she hissed.

Spinning to face him, she saw the guilt written all over his face as he winced. "You set me up."

He held his hands up as if to calm her, but she backed away. She didn't trust what she would do if he touched her right now. Rage was coursing through her, yet a little part of her couldn't help but note that he looked good. No, *hot*. Gone were the scrubs and the work clothes—instead, he was wearing jeans and a sweater beneath a dark leather jacket.

With a bit of a five o'clock shadow on that ridiculously cut jawline, he looked...*sexy. Dangerous*. She liked it. And her body liked it way too much. She was no longer sure if the rapid pulse and rising heat were due to anger or lust. Or both.

Oh hell, she was a mess.

He started to explain. "I know it was a bit underhanded, but you did promise to work with me on this."

She clenched her teeth and her fists, trying to restrain her emotions because, if she didn't, she had no idea if she would slap him or kiss him.

"And this will be a great opportunity to network with the right people," he continued. His low voice sounded so calm, so reasonable. Yup, she would definitely slap him.

The elevator came to a stop and she stormed out ahead of him. His hand on her arm stopped her before she could reach the front door of the lobby. Swinging around, she bit out, "What?"

His eyes were filled with a tenderness that nearly knocked her off her feet. Her breath left her lungs in an instant as he gazed down at her like she was the only woman on earth. Nope, she would definitely kiss him if she let herself go.

She tightened her fists until her nails dug into her palm, willing herself to keep control. "What?" she snapped again.

He sighed, his entire body seeming to deflate with disappointment. "I'm sorry," he said.

She studied him as he ran a hand through his unmussable hair. "I don't know what came over me. I just..." He shook his head. "I was desperate to see you."

His words combined with his self-deprecating laugh cut through her, threatening to dissolve her anger.

She had to get out of there before she did something stupid. Like let him off the hook. Or kiss him. Or throw herself into his arms like a drowning person searching for air, because that was exactly how she felt. Desperate and needy. As if she couldn't breathe, and moving closer to him was the only way to survive.

"Pick me up in two hours," she said. Spinning on her heel, she headed out the door, and hailed a cab.

They should have shared a cab since they were heading to the same place, but Alice couldn't fathom being alone in a tight space with him. Not now when she was this close to losing her grip on sanity. She needed space—room to breathe.

She had two hours to fortify herself, build back up her defenses so he couldn't get through.

* * * *

Two hours, two glasses of wine, and half a pint of ice cream later, and her shield was still not quite up to par. When he knocked on the door, her stomach felt wobbly, her heart jumping into her throat. *She could do this. It was one night.*

She could keep her cool—and her distance—for one freakin' night.

She opened the door and saliva pooled in her mouth. Oh sweet Jesus, he was so hot.

He was handsome in his work clothes, sexy and dangerous in his casual wear, but holy hell… The man was a stud in a suit. He'd shaved the five o'clock shadow and was standing in her doorway, looking ridiculously at ease in a perfectly tailored black suit.

He was eyeing her from head to toe just as she was studying him.

"You look gorgeous." His low voice made her shiver, and she tugged self-consciously at the hem of her silver cocktail dress.

It was her favorite formal dress—one that always made her feel confident and sexy.

So where was that confidence now when she needed it most?

An awkward silence loomed between them. Alice did not do awkward silences. She did not do awkward, period—except for anytime this particular man was around. Why? She wanted to yell at the injustice. At the complete insanity of it. But she held her yelling in check and backed up, allowing him into her home.

Unwanted memories from his last visit to her apartment flashed in her mind with a vengeance. Nicholas pressing her against the door as he kissed her senseless. The way his hands slid over her body, making her scream with pleasure. The way he'd felt pressed against her, the weight of his hard, naked body pressing her into the bed, making her feel safe…grounded.

Grounded? Where had that thought come from?

She blinked up at him, trying to shake off the memories. Maybe he was lost in the same train of thought because he was unusually quiet, his gaze fixed on her, dark and filled with promises. He took a step toward her and she told herself to move.

Her body did not listen.

She knew what would happen but she couldn't bring herself to stop it. She was frozen in place, partly horrified by what was about to occur, but also frighteningly eager.

He closed the distance between them in one step, pulling her close so she was pressed up against him. Her traitorous body pressed against his, her curves aching to mold to his hard strength.

That was all the encouragement he needed. One hand gently held the back of her neck as his lips moved over hers with a tender fierceness that made her tremble. Something in her chest cracked, and a sharp pain pierced her, begging to let go and let herself drown in this man's kisses. His gentle touch. His kind words.

She caught herself at the last minute, pushing him away from her with all her might even though it felt like defying gravity to break away from his embrace.

Taking two hasty steps back, she stopped when she hit the island in her little kitchen. She needed space. More room. She couldn't breathe.

Nicholas was breathing heavy, she noticed. But he was watching her with concern in his eyes. "Alice, I'm sorry—"

"No," she cut him off. "No, you're not sorry." Her voice shook with anger and other emotions she didn't want to name.

He must have heard it because his brows furrowed with concern. "Alice, please, let me—"

She shook her head, pushing off the counter and walking farther into the apartment to try to get some air. "I don't want to hear it. This was what you wanted, wasn't it? You made a big show out of inviting me to this event to *network*...."

He had the good grace to flinch at her sarcastic tone.

"When really, all you wanted was a way to get into my pants," she finished. "You're just like all the others." She hadn't meant for those words to slip out but they did, and the bitterness in her tone was impossible to ignore. It tainted the air around them like a toxic poison.

After a short silence, Nicholas ran his hand through his hair. "All the others?"

She pinched her lips together to keep from saying anymore. She'd already said too much. And really, what had she expected? She'd known all along that he was just another man. Sure, he did a good job of coming across as gallant and honorable, but deep down, he was just like every other man. Except that he was more dangerous because he hid it so well. She'd nearly come to believe that he was as genuine and honest as he seemed.

No one was that good. And no man did anything unless there was something in it for him. Like her. And it would be one thing if he just wanted her body—lots of men wanted that. That she could deal with. But he seemed to want more. He wanted all of her.

A shiver of fear had her rubbing her arms as she pushed past him to grab her wrap. When she turned back, he was standing where she'd left him, his eyes wide with surprise. She moved toward him, wrap and purse in hand, and took a deep breath before striding toward the door. "Shall we go?"

A light touch on her arm as she passed made her freeze in place.

"I don't understand," he said. "Shouldn't we talk about what just happened?"

She fixed her eyes on the door, unable to look him in the eyes. Her resolve was weak—part of her still wanted to throw herself into his arms and pick up where they had left off—but she clung to her will power desperately. "There's nothing to talk about. This is just business, right? Isn't that what you said?"

He didn't move his arm, and for a moment they stood there, touching but not looking at one another. Until finally, she heard him say quietly, "If that's what you want."

Her chest squeezed painfully, but she ignored it. "Let's go then."

Chapter 7

This was what he'd wanted, wasn't it? He should be thrilled. He had Alice on his arm—looking stunning in her formal gown and perfect hair and makeup. He'd won their little battle and had managed to get her out with him, on a date. Sort of.

The "sort of" was what made his smile feel forced as they walked through the door of the hotel's ballroom, brilliantly lit with chandeliers and twinkling lights, reflecting the holiday season and theme of the annual fundraiser.

They paused near the doorway, taking in the big band that played on stage, the whirling couples dancing around them, and the formally-attired wait staff who weaved through the crowd with their trays of appetizers. "What do you think?" he asked.

He looked down and saw Alice tilt her head to the side as she studied the scene before her. "I think this looks like every fundraiser or gala event I've ever been to."

He followed her gaze. She was right. He'd attended more than enough of these to last a lifetime, and they were always the same. The same people, the same elegant food and music, the same tepid vibe of polite laughter and inane small talk.

A wave of exhaustion swept over him at the thought of going through another one these nights. But then he looked down at his gorgeous date and grinned. Tonight would most definitely not be the same as any other night because he had her.

For tonight, at least.

As if she felt his gaze, she swung around to face him. "So, who should I meet first?" Her voice was clipped. Cold. Businesslike. "I'm thinking we should start over there where Mr. Jamison and his wife are. They could provide some great introductions."

He tried to ignore the bitter disappointment at her professional demeanor. Really, what had he expected? He'd all but forced him to come out with him tonight and all under the pretense of business. He couldn't really have expected that she would just forget that—lose herself to the date-like atmosphere.

But the utter disappointment that had him scowling at the crowd told him he had done just that. He'd hoped she'd forget about business—not entirely, of course, they had a job to do. But enough so that he could get to know her. Enough that her thick wall of defenses might lower for just a bit.

He nodded. "Sure, that's as good a place to start as any."

But they didn't get far. "Hey, Hot Doc!"

Alice froze in place when he groaned. He looked down to see her biting her lip, her eyes bright with laughter. "*Hot Doc?*"

He opened his mouth to explain, but it was too late. Claudia had reached them, Frank just behind her giving him an apologetic grimace. Claudia smiled at him, but her attention was quickly distracted by Alice. Her eyes rounded, and she made no attempt to hide the fact that she was openly assessing his date… *Colleague*, he mentally corrected.

She let out a little whistle. "Well, I can see why Nicholas is so smitten."

Nicholas dropped his head into in hand and rubbed his eyes wearily. Of course his best friend would humiliate him. Why had he expected anything less?

His head shot up again at the sound of Alice's soft laugh. It was genuine laughter, not her forced laugh she used around her boss. Since when did he know her different laughs? She was smiling at Claudia—a *real* smile. "Alice," she said.

Claudia reached for her hand with an answering grin. "I know. I've heard all about you."

Alice raised an eyebrow, but she looked amused. "Then I'm the one at a loss here. You are…?"

"Oh, right." Nicholas remembered his duties. "Sorry, Alice. This is Claudia. She's a cardiovascular surgeon at the hospital."

Claudia put her hands on her hips and tilted her head to the side, so he added, "She's also my best friend."

Was it his imagination, or did Alice's posture relax slightly? Had she been jealous? He shook his head—now he was just being hopeful.

"I'm glad to finally meet the infamous Alice," Claudia said, stepping next to Alice and taking her arm like they were long-lost friends. To his surprise, Alice didn't back away or turn on her chilly, standoffish persona he'd come to know. She laughed at the description. "Infamous, huh? That doesn't sound good."

Claudia shrugged one shoulder. "Well, you are the one who loved him and left him."

He watched Alice's jaw drop, and her wide eyes shot to his. He winced at the accusation he saw there. Yes, he'd told Claudia about their night together—and her cold dismissal the next the morning. *But she was his best friend*, he wanted to say. Before he could make any excuses, Claudia barreled on.

"Oh, don't be mad at Nick. He had to talk to someone about it."

Alice's jaw snapped shut and she turned to look at Claudia. She didn't say anything, but Nicholas could have sworn he saw curiosity in her eyes.

"It isn't every day that a woman rejects our fine doctor here," his best friend said, as if he wasn't standing right next to them. "As you can imagine, he's pretty in-demand with the ladies."

Alice let out a short laugh. "I can imagine."

Claudia nodded sagely. "But..." She leaned over and spoke in a faux whisper that he and Frank could clearly hear. "I am here to tell you that he's never acted like this with any woman. Ever."

He was about to protest. A man's pride could only take so much. But to his surprise, Alice's cheeks turned a fetching shade of pink. Was she... Was she *blushing*?

"Oh no?" she murmured.

Claudia shook her head and gave Alice's arm a pat like she was her little sister or something. She dropped the teasing tone. "I know he went about inviting you tonight the *entirely* wrong way, but trust me. I've known him for a long time, and this is a first. He's normally the one being chased." She leaned in as if sharing a secret. "I mean they don't call him 'Hot Doc' for nothing."

Alice let out a loud laugh. "Hot Doc, I love it."

Nicholas felt the need to interject. "No one but Claudia calls me that." But neither of the women paid him any attention.

"He hates it," Claudia admitted.

Alice's grin was wicked. "Even better."

Claudia turned to him then. "So, you two have any awesome revelations yet?"

He couldn't bring himself to tear his eyes away from Alice and that mischievous grin. "Hmm?"

"Your fundraiser, remember? Have you gotten any great inspiration from the gala?" Claudia asked.

Oh, right. Business. That's why there were here. Before he could respond, Alice intervened. "What do you think of this gala, Claudia?"

Claudia looked around them and sighed. "Same old, same old."

"Exactly," Alice said so quietly he almost didn't hear her.

He turned to Frank to try to bring him into the conversation—the consummate introvert; he hated these kind of parties more than any of them. But before he could, he heard Claudia whisper to Alice, "You know those women I was telling you about? The ones who like to chase our Hot Doc here? Well, prepare to meet one of the most ruthless."

He turned to see Marla Reese headed in their direction. A young, wealthy divorcee, she had indeed set her sights on him a couple of years ago. But after a few polite conversations in which he explained he wasn't interested, she had let it go gracefully. Though she did like to flirt at these type of society functions, she was hardly on the prowl. He gave Claudia a questioning look over Alice's head, and she met his look with a small smile and a little wink.

When Marla approached, she gave him her typically effusive hug and kissed both his cheeks, ensuring he's been branded with her hot pink lipstick. "Marla, good to see you," he said as he tried to surreptitiously wipe his face with the back of his hand.

"Nicky," she said. "I didn't think you'd be here tonight. I'm so happy you could make it."

He heard Alice's snicker at the nickname but ignored it. "Marla, you and your committee did a lovely job with the entertainment tonight."

Marla beamed at the praise.

He half turned to Alice. "May I introduce you to my, er—" He paused, unsure of what to call her. He had a feeling the word "date" would not go over well with Alice. He was about to say, "Colleague," but Marla cut him off, her eyes never so much as glancing in Alice's direction.

"I think it's so wonderful that you're spearheading the new children's clinic," she said, her voice as breathless as ever. "My friends and I were just saying how noble it was of you to lead up this charity project."

Noble. The word made his stomach churn with a mixture of guilt and disgust. It wasn't "charity," it was a necessary service for an underserved population that was facing ridiculously high health care premiums. And it was hardly noble. Yes, he'd helped to promote the new clinic to the board and the donors, but it wasn't as though his intentions were entirely selfless. Part of him had done it because it was the right thing to do. But the new clinic's timing had also coincided nicely with his five-year plan. If everything went according to plan—and it almost always did thanks to his meticulous planning—the head of pediatrics position at the Boston branch would be his. If that happened, he wouldn't even have a chance to step foot in the new clinic. But before he could say any of that, Marla continued the conversation without him. "I do hope you'll save me a dance later, Nicky."

Again, he opened his mouth to reply but didn't have the chance. To his surprise, he felt Alice's hand on his upper arm.

"If you'll excuse us, Marla," she said, her voice a low purr of polite subtext. "Nicky and I were just about to head out to the dance floor." She looked up at him then, her eyes filled with an emotion he recognized but didn't dare to believe.

"Isn't that right, *Nicky?*" she added.

He nodded mutely, afraid that if he opened his mouth he would laugh out loud. Giving a little wave of good-bye to his friends, he saw Claudia give him a thumbs-up as Alice practically dragged him onto the dance floor.

Was it his imagination or had she been jealous?

* * * *

Alice barely saw the dancers as she weaved her way through the crowd, Nicholas in tow. She was too focused on repeating the same mantra over and over. *She was not jealous. There was no way in hell she was jealous. She couldn't be jealous.*

She turned to face Nicholas and let him scoop her into his arms as a slow dance began. Trying not to notice the way her body responded to his, she kept her gaze focused on his chin. Yes, the cleft was adorable, but it was far better than getting sucked into those eyes. That had been her undoing earlier in the night. She'd let the innate sexual tension between them get out of hand.

Glancing over his shoulder she saw the glamorously awful Marla watching them, her lips pursed in an unbecoming scowl. And she wasn't the only one. Alice had been keenly aware of the myriad of women whose faces had lit up upon seeing Nicholas—and then fallen flat when they'd spotted her on his arm.

That was not sweet satisfaction that had her lips twitching up into a smile. Absolutely not.

Nicholas led them with a sort of innate grace that made her feel weightless. His head dipped down toward hers. "You know there's nothing going on between me and Marla."

Her eyes shot up from his chin to his eyes. Dammit, she'd forgotten her vow to avoid looking into those blue pools of kindness.

"So?" She sounded like a bratty teen, but she couldn't seem to help it. His lips pressed together, and she had the infuriating sensation that he was struggling not to laugh.

The shoulder beneath her hand lifted in a small shrug. "It's just that you seemed a bit put out by her…uh…attentions."

Alice clenched her teeth to hold back a catty remark. *She was not jealous, goddammit!*

"I just wanted to dance," she bit out.

"Mmm." His murmured acknowledgment did not sound convinced but she refused to fight him on it. The more she protested, the worse she would look. So instead, she did what she'd sworn she'd do tonight—she focused on business.

"Have you noticed that no one seems especially psyched to be here?" It was the thought she'd been stewing over since they'd walked through the door. She loved a good party, and she loved a reason to dress up even more, but even she'd had the urge to yawn when they'd walked in the door.

Nicholas's lopsided grin made her mouth water. *Shit. She would start drooling soon if she didn't stay focused.*

"Did you expect people to be *psyched*?" he asked, over-enunciating her childish word choice.

She rolled her eyes, ignoring his teasing. "Shouldn't they be? I mean this is supposed to be a party. The donors are presumably coming out to have fun, and in exchange they lighten their wallets."

He gave a little nod. "I guess." His arms tightened around her, drawing her closer, and she found herself holding her breath.

Work. They were here for work.

She focused on the adorable indentation in his chin. "I'm serious, Nicholas. You heard Claudia—this is the same old, same old. If we really want to wow the board and my boss, we need to think outside the box. We need to do something different. Daring."

She glanced up then and it was a mistake. His eyes were fixed on her, and they were filled with so much undisguised desire that knocked the wind out of her. She lost her footing and stumbled into him.

The contact was brief but electric. Her chest pressed to his, his arms tight around her waist as he caught her to him to keep her from falling. Their faces were inches apart, his lips so close, her head tilted up.

Oh God, she wanted him to kiss her more than anything in the world.

She could feel his chest rise and fall with his ragged breathing, his hands clenching into the fabric of her dress with a desperate desire that had her lips parting for air. And for his kiss. She wouldn't stop him, couldn't turn away if she wanted to. She needed his lips against hers like she needed to breathe.

"Nicholas! Yoo-hoo, Dr. Bale!"

The sound of a woman calling his name brought her back to reality. Finding her footing, she pressed against him, forcing him to loosen his grip as they both turned to face the bubbly brunette who was headed their way with a megawatt smile and a skintight dress.

Once again, Alice was completely ignored as the woman came toward them, her eyes fixed on Nicholas and her perfect curls bobbing as she moved. "Why, Nicholas, I didn't know you were going to be here tonight," she crooned.

Alice gritted her teeth. *She was not jealous, she could not be jealous.*

But she could be thoroughly annoyed that this woman had inconsiderately barged in on their dance—and more importantly, their conversation.

What conversation? The only conversation about to take place was between two tongues.

She silenced her inner critic. They had been discussing work before she'd tripped and before they'd been so rudely interrupted.

Nicholas laughed at something the bimbo was saying, and Alice inhaled deeply as the brunette took that laugh as a cue to reach out and touch his forearm, leaning over far enough that he and everyone else in the near vicinity could see her ample cleavage.

Work. She was here for work. The fact that Nicholas was flirting with another woman had nothing to do with her. Not that he was outright flirting, per se, but still—his old-school chivalry and charming manners were catnip for women, as he must have known. They all wanted him. She glanced around the room, taking note of all the women who were subtly watching Nicholas's every move.

And that was when it clicked. The answer to their dilemma. The majority of these patrons were either women or men who had been dragged along by their wives. She had to assume the patrons for the children's clinic would be the same demographic.

And what did they all have in common? They wanted Nicholas. And who could blame them? Sexy, handsome, chivalrous, well-dressed, and a doctor to boot? The guy was the closest thing to a real-life Prince Charming she'd ever seen. Add to that the fact that he apparently loved children and had a heart of gold and the man was a walking wet dream for women.

Excitement had her heart racing for an entirely different reason than it had been a moment before. As the idea took hold, the excitement replaced the jealousy—okay, so maybe she'd been a little jealous. But now she was fixed. She'd focused on work, and it had not only worked to distract her—she'd had a brilliant idea.

By the time he said his good-byes to the brunette, Alice was fidgeting with unrestrained excitement, her hands clenching together to resist tugging on Nicholas's sleeve like an overeager child.

Alice didn't pay attention to what Nicholas was saying to the young woman, but whatever it was, it was a very polite brush-off, if the woman's slightly perplexed expression was anything to go by. She almost pitied the woman as they watched her turn and sashay away, off to find another single, attractive, successful, and kind male doctor. Because they were a dime a dozen—*not*. But that was what made her idea so brilliant!

He turned toward her, his head slightly ducked as he scratched the back of his neck, clearly embarrassed by the attention. "Sorry about that," he started.

"Don't be," Alice interrupted.

"Yeah but we were in the middle of a dance—"

Alice couldn't wait any longer. She shot her hand out and grabbed his arm. "I have an idea."

He looked down at her hand on his arm and then back up to her eyes, which she was sure were frighteningly wide and filled with an evangelical zeal.

"What's your idea?" he asked warily.

Barely able to contain her excitement, she blurted it out. "I know how we can make this fundraiser a huge success. You. It's all about you."

His brows drew together, his eyes scrunched up in confusion. "Me?"

She exhaled loudly. Dammit, she wasn't explaining this well. She was too excited to slow down. *Just cut to the chase.* She inhaled quickly and spit it out in one breath. "I want to auction you off to the highest bidder."

* * * *

Nicholas looked down at his stunningly gorgeous date and tried to make sense out of the words that were coming out of her luscious mouth. Maybe it was an overdose of desire that was making him hard of hearing because he could have sworn she'd said... He cleared his throat. "Excuse me?"

"A bachelor auction," she said. Her voice was breathless with excitement. Her eyes glowing in the dim ballroom lighting. He was so distracted by the change in her that he almost didn't register the words that were coming out of her mouth.

A bachelor auction. His stomach twisted in revulsion at the mere name. "No. Uh-uh." He shook his head and tried not to be swayed by her pleading gaze.

"Just hear me out. This could be perfect. Women love you. I mean, seriously, look around you—"

He did look around just then and noticed that they were garnering stares from nearby dancers. Smiling at an older couple he recognized from past functions, he took Alice by the elbow and steered her toward the edge of the dance floor. He could only hope no one had overheard what she'd been saying.

She didn't seem to notice that she was being escorted off the dance floor, she kept talking, her face turned up to his. Her lips so close and so tempting that it was difficult to breathe let alone concentrate on the words that were coming out of her mouth.

"It's perfect," she was saying as they reached a semi-secluded corner. Her hands gripped his arms and the light touch was enough to addle his senses and render him temporarily speechless.

Jesus, he was in over his head with this woman. For a man who lived by logic and plans, she was an anomaly. The effect she had on him was a mystery. But he loved it.

It was insanity. Not just her idea—though that, too—but this reaction he had to her. It was stronger than all the rigid plans he'd set his life course to—the methodology that had run his life, quite effectively at that, since he was in middle school. Whatever this was between them, it had completely thrown him off course, had overthrown everything he'd thought he'd known, and had him feeling his way blindly like a man stumbling in the dark. For the first time in his life, he was utterly and completely lost.

How did she not feel it?

He half-listened as she described in detail the way that she would auction off a number of single male hospital employees—but he would be the highlight. The key feature. *Because women loved him*, he heard her say.

Her eyes still bright with excitement, he watched her case the room as if looking for proof. "All of these women," she said, gesturing to the crowd, "they all want you."

All except you. She was talking about women in general. Not her. Apparently his date, whom he'd hoped to be wooing, was ready to auction him off to someone else. Literally. He didn't know whether to laugh or shout. This woman was not only pushing him away, she was selling him off!

And yet, he was still standing here watching her with dazed fascination. He couldn't help it. Despite all of her attempts to keep him at bay, despite the forced coldness and the brick wall she put up around him—he was smitten. That was the only word he could think to describe it.

This was an infatuation, surely, but whatever it was, it was a first.

Maybe Claudia had a point; maybe he was just intrigued by the chase. It was possible he'd be able to move on if he just had a chance to get to know her. It was the mystery that had him so enamored. Her shifting responses, the flickers of genuine emotions he caught sight of behind her well-maintained cool façade—that was what intrigued him. He wanted—no, needed—to get to know the woman whose laugh filled him with life, the woman who'd cried on his shoulder over her elderly neighbor friend, the woman whose intelligence sparkled in her eyes, as undeniable as her physical beauty. There was so much more to her than what she showed the world, and from the glimpses he'd seen, he liked it. He liked her.

"What do you think?" she asked. She blinked up at him, lips parted slightly.

He could kiss her. It had almost happened on the dance floor, and he knew without a doubt that she'd wanted it, too. He could kiss her now and silence this whole ridiculous conversation.

But he knew exactly what would happen if he did that. She would respond to him physically at first, but once her senses returned, she'd pull away. Or worse, she'd run from him. This seemed to be the pattern with them—one he was determined to break. He just had no idea how.

She was waiting for an answer, and he thrust a hand through his hair as he told her the truth. "I don't want to do it."

Some of the excitement drained from her face and he had to fight the inexplicable guilt. She was asking him to sell himself…in public…to a bunch of women who he tried to avoid on a regular basis. Why the hell did he feel guilty?

Maybe because that genuine excitement he saw in her eyes was so honest and sweet…and rare. He wanted to see this side of her all the time.

"I thought you wanted this event to be a success," she said, crossing her arms over her chest—apparently not realizing how distracting her exposed cleavage looked in that particular pose. He forced his gaze up to meet hers before he did something crazy like pull her into his arms and kiss her senseless.

"I do want this to be a success," he said. "But—"

"You've got to admit that it's a good idea," she continued. She leaned in toward him in her eagerness, and her soft vanilla scent surrounded him making it difficult to think. God, he wanted to kiss her so badly it hurt.

"It's one night," she continued. "Just one night. And it's not like I'm asking you to marry the winner or anything, the prize will be a date. How hard could that be?"

He could barely hear her words anymore. He was supposed to be smart, driven, strong-willed. So how was it that this woman reduced him to a pile of idiocy just by talking to him? What was she saying? *How hard could a date be?*

And that's when it occurred to him—a stroke of genius in the midst of his brain's current timeout. "I'll do it." The words came out before he could properly think this through. But this could be his one chance to get to know her. It was worth a shot.

Her eyes widened with surprise, but then she graced him with a smile that was so genuine, so beautiful he was nearly too stunned to get the next words out. "On one condition."

Her smile froze, and he could hear his heart pounding in the brief silence that followed his statement. He saw her tighten her arms across her chest as if preparing physically. "Go on," she said.

He cleared his throat and glanced around the crowded ballroom to make sure no one was listening. It was pathetic enough that he was resorting to extortion to get a date, he didn't need witnesses.

"I'll be your star bachelor at the event…if you agree to let me date you."

Her jaw dropped open, and her eyes went frighteningly blank.

"Just until the event," he said. "And if you never want to see me again after that, I will leave you alone. I just want a chance—"

The blank expression vanished as her lips turned down in a scowl. "Let me get this straight. You'll do your part to make *your* event a success… *if I sleep with you?*"

The coldness in her voice made his heart clench. "Jesus, Alice, no!" He took a step toward her and flinched when she backed away.

His brain scrambled to make this right. "I just meant date. Like two people going out and getting to know each other. I didn't mean sex. Geez, Alice, is that what dating means to you?"

The instant the words left his mouth, he wished he could call them back.

Her cheeks turned pink and her lips clamped shut, but he couldn't tell if she was angry or embarrassed.

Dammit, he was making a mess of this. He reached out toward her but again she shrank back. "Look, I'm sorry. I didn't mean that, and I didn't mean to offend you."

A silence fell between them, and he watched her shoulders loosen slightly at the apology.

He took a deep breath and tried again, softening his tone and stepping back so he was no longer looming over her. All of his excuses and rationalizations for wanting this arrangement flew through his head, but somehow he knew that trying to justify himself would only make this work. So he stuck with the simple, honest truth. "I like you."

Her gaze met his before darting toward the front door. Was that panic he saw in her eyes? He resisted the urge to reach out and hold on to her to keep her from fleeing.

"I like you," he said again. "And I just want a chance to get to know you. Is that so bad?"

* * * *

Is that so bad? A hysterical laugh started to rise in her throat, and she clamped her mouth shut to keep it locked inside. Is that so bad? *Yes!*

But this man—this honest, genuine, kind man—was looking at her with such tenderness, such caring—how the hell could she explain it to him? He would never understand.

She'd *dated*, for lack of a better word, musicians and bikers and even a guy who had ties to the mob. But none of them were as dangerous as this sexy doctor. Everything about the guy from his clean-cut hairstyle to his square jaw with the adorable cleft cried "Prince Charming." But she *knew* better. The gallant, chivalrous, noble hero only existed in fairytales and black-and-white movies. He was not real.

I like you. The words rang in her ears, disarmingly simple, but their effect on her was anything but.

Maybe because she liked him back. She shook her head slightly, trying to shove aside the thought, but her conscience wouldn't let her lie to herself. She *did* like him. Or at least, she liked what little she knew of him. She liked the way he remembered the assistants' names at the office. Or how he spent time with Ena, a woman he barely knew, and had kept her company while she was in the hospital. Or the way he held doors open for her like he'd just stepped out of one of her old movies. And she liked the way he looked at her—like he was looking at her right now—like she was the only person on the planet, despite the fact that there were dozens of other women in the room, all of whom were trying to get his attention.

He was watching her reaction now, and the concern in his gaze brought her back to the first night they'd met. He'd been so confident and calm when she'd been flipping out. And not only that, but also the way he'd been after the fact. The way he'd held her in his arms as she'd cried and hadn't run in the opposite direction at the sight of her emotions. More than that—she'd known he would stay with her. He was just so reliable, so trustworthy, so...not what she'd expected.

That was why she liked him—and that was what made him more dangerous than any guy she'd ever met.

She started to shake her head, but before she could say the word "no" he started speaking.

"What if I promise not to make any moves?" He raised his brows in a hopeful look that was so cute it hurt her heart. "I promise not to take advantage of you in any way."

Alice couldn't stop the choked laugh that escaped her lips. It wasn't him she was worried about. No more than five minutes ago, she'd been just about ready to throw herself into this man's arms, heedless of the consequences or the audience around them.

He leaped on her temporary silence. "What have you got to lose?"

Everything. The thought was completely irrational, but she couldn't silence it. She didn't want to like this man any more than she already did. She didn't want to get to know him, and she sure as hell didn't want him to know her.

Liar.

Okay, so maybe she did. And was it any wonder? The guy was the whole package. He was like one of her old movie crushes come to life. Hell, the man had just *waltzed* with her, for God's sake. But it would lead to trouble.

He was watching her, waiting for her answer. She should say no. But his gaze was so sweet, so hopeful. She found herself saying, "I'll think about it."

She was rewarded with a huge grin, complete with dimples and a cleft that would have made any model proud. He reached out and grabbed her hand. "Come on, let's have another dance—uninterrupted this time, I promise."

When she resisted the tug on her hand, he leaned down and whispered teasingly, "One dance. I'll even let you tell me about this ridiculous bachelor auction you've got planned."

She let herself be dragged onto the dance floor even as her brain told her to shut this down. *Later*, she promised herself. She would tell him no later, after they'd had a bit of fun and she'd managed to convince him of the brilliance of her plan. He would get on board, and then she would break it to him that she had no intention of dating him. Ever.

But she would just enjoy one harmless dance first.

Chapter 8

One dance turned into two, and as they moved across the dance floor. Nicholas was oblivious to the crowd around them, completely transfixed by the sweet, dreamy smile that Alice wore. He almost didn't want to interrupt whatever trance she was in, but he found himself too curious to hold out any longer. "What are you thinking about?"

Her head tilted back so she was looking into his eyes, but she didn't lose the smile. God, he loved that smile. It spoke of a sweetness and innocence that was completely at odds with the hardened, poised façade she normally presented.

"Hmmm?" Even her voice sounded dreamy.

He couldn't risk pulling her out of this state, so he changed tactics. Leaning down, he said quietly in her ear, "You're a wonderful dancer."

Her cheeks flushed, and her eyes dropped down. "Thank you."

He thought she wouldn't speak anymore, but then, she blurted out, "I used to want to be a dancer."

The words should not have been a bombshell. But they were. This was the first time she'd ever willingly offered up personal information about herself, and he had the feeling he was walking on eggshells as he maneuvered her into a turn.

He chose his words carefully, hoping his eagerness wasn't readily apparent. "What made you want to dance?"

Her eyes flickered up to his, and he caught the wariness there, as though he'd just asked her to divulge her bank account information rather than a simple question about her childhood. What the hell had happened to this woman that she was so wary of men?

He had enough experience with wary children with a massive distrust of doctors to know that pushing the issue would only make it worse. The best thing he could do was offer up something about himself, let her get to know him before asking her to trust him. "I always wanted to be a doctor."

Her eyes widened slightly at the change of topic, but she didn't respond, so he continued. "My father was a doctor, and his father before him. I guess I always knew that it was what I was meant to do."

One corner of her mouth turned up at that. "That must be nice," she said. "To be so certain of where you stand in the world—where you're meant to be."

Her words struck a chord. She was right—he had always known his place in the world. He'd always had it all mapped out. First it had been mapped out for him by his parents, and then he'd taken over the obsessive planning that seemed inherent in his genes. He'd never lost track of his path—until he met this woman. She was not part of the plan. He was supposed to fall in love with a woman who loved him back and who fit in with the lifestyle that he'd created. It was supposed to be easy.

For the first time in his life, the plan wasn't working. Oh, his career was right on track—when this fundraiser was a success, there was no doubt he'd be offered the position. He was already the frontrunner according to his friends on the board. But that eventual coup no longer held the same appeal it had before. It seemed...hollow. Lonely.

But that was ridiculous. He'd gone into this wife-hunting plan solely to reach the next step in his life plan, not out of any sense of loneliness or need. But now...now that he'd met someone who filled a void he hadn't known existed, the idea of not having it in his life made him achingly aware of the gaping hole in his life where love should be.

She was watching him closely, and he got the sense she saw more in his expression than he would have liked, so he forced a smile and was as truthful as possible. "It was nice. It *is* nice," he clarified. "But knowing what you want to do as a profession isn't the same as knowing where you fit in the world. Or with whom."

Her smile faltered a bit, and she tilted her head to the side. "I guess that's true. I'm glad I found my niche in PR, though," she said. "I can't imagine doing anything else."

"Not even dancing?" he teased. She rolled her eyes, but she was still smiling, so he pushed it a bit further. "What type of dancer did you want to be? A ballerina?" He couldn't help but grin at the image of a little red-haired girl with a tutu and Alice's now-familiar look of determination.

But Alice shook her head. "Oh no, I never took ballet lessons or anything like that." She paused briefly, but then she said, "I wanted to be a ballroom dancer."

He moved back slightly so he could see her face better. "Seriously? A ballroom dancer?"

She nodded quickly, her lips pressed together in what looked like an attempt not to laugh out loud.

"Now I'm *really* intrigued," he said in all seriousness. "Where did that idea come from?"

She let out the laugh then and the sound was more beautiful than the orchestra's playing. He had a feeling that sound—her real, genuine laugh—was only heard by a rare few. And God help him if he didn't want to be in that exclusive club.

She shook her head, still laughing. "I know. It's a weird dream for a kid to have. But my sister and I…" She hesitated for a second but finally continued. "We used to love old movies. Still do, I guess. But my favorites were always the musicals." When she looked up at him, her eyes wide and guileless, he almost lost his footing.

"You know, the Fred and Ginger ones?" she said.

He nodded mutely, afraid that if he spoke she would clam up on him again.

She shrugged. "I know it's stupid but—"

"It's not stupid."

Her head shot up, and he realized he'd sounded a bit too gruff. Too intense. He tried to soften it a bit. "It's not stupid. It was a childhood dream." He leaned in a bit. "I bet you would have made an incredible ballroom dancer."

Her cheeks turned pink again, but she held his gaze for a moment before glancing down at the two of them moving in time with the music. "Well, for now I have to settle for dancing at fundraisers with handsome doctors."

The surge of pleasure that coursed through him at the compliment was absurd. He heard more profuse compliments on a daily basis—but still, it was heartening. "I'm no Fred Astaire…."

She laughed and tilted her head back, and he caught sight of the mischievous glimmer in her eyes. "You're no Fred Astaire," she agreed. "But you'll do."

It could barely even be considered a compliment, yet those words stayed with him for the rest of the evening. They gave him hope as he escorted Alice to the bar, deftly maneuvering them so they avoided the more aggressive admirers in attendance.

With champagne in hand, he steered her toward a secluded corner, hoping against hope that he could lure her into another conversation. Once they were settled, he asked, "So how did you and your sister discover this love of old movies?"

And just like that, the glimpse of the real Alice was gone. He saw the shutters come down in her eyes as she took a sip of her champagne and turned to look at the dancers on the dance floor. "We should talk some more about this bachelor auction," she said.

His stomach fell. Somehow he'd asked the wrong question, and her walls were back up. Not only that, but she was back on the topic of his humiliation. Fantastic.

He went along with it with a sigh. "All right. Assuming you agree to my terms, what exactly did you have in mind."

She went into full-blown sales mode then, and Nicholas found himself warming to the plan—he still hated that he'd be selling himself to the highest bidder—but he couldn't help but admit that it was a good idea. It would be something new for the jaded socialites and bored Upper East Side wives who were their biggest donors.

Her eyes bright with excitement, Alice used her hands as she was talking, gesturing wildly in her enthusiasm.

It was no wonder she was the rising star of her company. Dixon had told him that, and it was a no-brainer. She was ambitious, fearless, and clearly passionate about what she did.

"How did you get into PR?" he asked.

She blinked at him for a moment, as she adjusted to the change of topic. She shrugged. "I fell into it, I guess."

Something told him there was more to it than that, but those damned walls were still firmly in place. So he tried a different tact. Maybe if he worked with her on this ridiculous event, she would open up again, overcome whatever foot-in-mouth comment he'd unwittingly made before. "So, what's the venue you're imagining?" He looked around the ballroom. "Something like this?"

Her nose wrinkled up as she followed his gaze. "No," she said. "I don't think so. This type of setting has been overdone. We need something different, something…"

Her eyes took on a faraway look that he was beginning to recognize. She was brainstorming… And it was adorable.

The moment was interrupted, however, when her purse started to buzz. He watched her fumble through the tiny handbag's contents before she pulled out her phone. Her face paled noticeably when she read whatever it said, and Nicholas found himself instinctively reaching out, wrapping an arm around her shoulder. "What is it?"

When she looked up, the real Alice was back—but not because she was caught up in dancing or because he'd wooed her into a conversation. No, he saw genuine emotion all right, but this time it was sheer panic.

* * * *

Alice's brain went blank for a moment. Life turned upside down. "My sister," she said through frozen lips. "She's in the hospital."

Nicholas. Thank God for Nicholas. He was the epitome of calm. Just like the night they'd first met, she watched him transform into a cool, capable doctor. Lowering himself a bit, he was at eye level as he asked her a series of questions. She realized dimly that he thought her sister had been in a car accident or something—he was asking questions about her status that made no sense.

"She went into labor." The words came out quickly, and she watched the sudden, almost comical change in Nicholas as they sank in. She waited for him to calm her, to tell her she had nothing to worry about, women gave birth all the time. But instead, he lightly gripped her elbow and started steering her toward the door.

"What are we waiting for? You want to be with your sister, don't you?"

Yes! Yes. More than anything, she wanted to see for herself that her sister was all right. She didn't have any weird fears about giving birth but the fact of the matter was—her sister was in the hospital. That's all that seemed to matter.

Twenty excruciatingly long minutes later their cab dropped them off at Nicholas's hospital. They reached the waiting room, and Alice spotted her friends through the glass doors.

She turned back quickly before Nicholas could enter. "You don't have to stick around."

He ignored her, giving her a little smirk of disbelief before leading the way into the waiting room.

Her friends looked up and rushed toward her the moment she stepped inside, and Alice temporarily forgot about her date. Caitlyn reached her first, and Alice fell into her hug. Meg and Caitlyn had been friends since freshman year of college, and she loved Meg almost as much as she did. When Alice drew back she saw Caitlyn staring over her shoulder at Nicholas with comically wide eyes. *Geez, be more obvious, Cait.* She spotted Ben over Caitlyn's shoulder, and he gave her a wink that made her smile, despite the cold pit of fear that had lodged itself in her chest.

"Jake is in there with her," Caitlyn said in a rush, apparently over her fascination with Alice's tux-clad date. "But he's been coming out every once in a while to give us updates. So far Meg and the baby are doing great."

Alice nodded. She waited for the fear to dissipate but there was no relief. Her sister was fine; Caitlyn just said so.

Still, until she saw Meg and the baby with her own eyes—preferably far, far away from a hospital setting, she knew she wouldn't be able to relax.

Caitlyn stepped aside and Alice moved past her to hug Tamara and Marc, her roommate, who were patiently waiting their turn. Once the niceties were dispensed with, Tamara launched into her story of how Meg went into labor while working at the bar.

Alice cursed under her breath at her sister's stubbornness. She and Jake had tried to veer her away from the manual labor these past couple months, but her sister hated to feel useless and had insisted on working right on up until the moment the baby was born. It looked like she'd gotten her wish.

As Tamara talked, Alice noticed Marc staring over her shoulder. When Tamara trailed off, he whispered loudly, "Who. Is. That?"

Alice didn't have to look back to know who had him stunned. Marc had an eye for beautiful men, and there was no doubt in her mind that her friend was stunned into reverent whispers at the sight of the oh-so-classically-handsome doctor.

Who was still here, it seemed, despite her hints that he should leave. Rather than annoyance, she felt a flood of relief. She didn't need him here, but she couldn't deny that he was a calming influence—there was something so unshakeable about him. So grounded. Especially in a hospital setting.

Marc and Tamara—and no doubt Caitlyn and Ben, who were standing to her left—were waiting for an introduction. "You guys, this is Dr. Nicholas Bale," she said, not turning to see his reaction, which she was positive was charming and kind, because that's just how he was. All the time. It was freakin' annoying.

She heard Tamara and Marc introduce themselves before turning to whisper to one another. Somehow she had a feeling Meg had told them all about the mysterious doctor at the theater gala and the pieces were clicking together for her friends. Let them think what they would. She would explain the truth to them on Saturday morning at the next Operation Petticoat gathering.

What was more unusual was the awkward silence that fell when it was Caitlyn's turn to introduce herself. Alice looked to her friend and saw that she was a bright pink as she gave Nicholas a little wave. "Hi again," she said.

She snapped her head to the side to see Nicholas giving Caitlyn a sweet, knowing smile that made her want to rip someone's eyes out. "Hey, Caitlyn, good to see you."

"You guys know each other?" she blurted out, just as Ben stepped up and wrapped a possessive arm around Caitlyn's waist. So she wasn't the only one who picked up on the awkwardness apparently.

Caitlyn turned to her, ignoring the question and Nicholas. "Jake said it's going to be a while. Like, a *while*-while. Ben and I are going to head home and come back first thing in the morning."

Alice nodded and returned Caitlyn's hug.

"Call me if you need anything," Caitlyn said as she and Ben headed toward the exit hand in hand.

Tamara and Marc followed shortly after with similar promises to return first thing in the morning, and leaving her alone with Nicholas—her date.

He stepped up beside her and placed an arm around her shoulders. "This is exciting, you know." His voice was gentle, teasing—and for some reason it seemed to unlock the emotions she'd been shoving aside since the text came in, and she found herself once again battling tears in front of this man.

She gave a jerky nod. It was exciting. Of course it was. At the end of all this, her sister would have her dream come true—her baby, her miracle. The family she'd always wanted and never had. Maybe finally someone in their family would get it right. If there was anyone who could excel at the parenting thing, it was Meg. And Jake, for that matter.

She should be excited. She *would* be excited—once she knew her sister was okay.

As if reading her mind, Nicholas leaned over again and said softly, "Would it make you feel better if I go check on your sister's progress with her doctor?"

Alice nodded quickly. Yes. *Yes, yes, yes.* She didn't know Meg's doctor personally, but she trusted Nicholas. If he said she was all right, if he thought there was nothing to worry about—maybe then she could relax. Maybe some of this fear would dissipate.

"Yes, please," she whispered. He disappeared down a hallway, and she found herself letting out a long breath of relief that he was on top of things. Her Nicholas—so strong, so collected, so...capable.

Her Nicholas? She shook her head in disgust. Since when had she started to think of him as *her* anything? And the fact that she had come to trust him—had come to rely on him even...

She should have been horrified. She *would* have been horrified if she wasn't so preoccupied with her sister's condition. But she would deal with that issue tomorrow, once her sister and her baby were safe and sound at home. Away from this hospital. In the meantime... She looked around the sterile waiting room and tried to fight the panic that always threatened to overwhelm her in hospitals. In the meantime, she would do whatever she had to do to get through this night. And if that meant giving in to her weakness and relying on Nicholas for the time being—so be it.

He came back into the room then, and she tried to ignore her heart's flip-flop in her chest. It was just the nerves talking. Just the anxiety. He was a doctor, of course she would be happy to see him here. This was purely practical.

"How is she?" she asked the moment he reached her side.

His smile was warm, comforting. Was it any wonder so many of his female acquaintances seemed to be head over heels in love? If he smiled at all of them this way, it was his own fault.

"She's doing great," he said. Wrapping one arm around her, he steered her toward a seat and gently eased her into it, taking the seat next to hers.

Relief made her knees shaky, and she was grateful for the help. Shit, she hated hospitals.

"You know, a lot of people would be excited right now," he said in a tone so casual and teasing it jarred her out of her thoughts.

She blinked up at him. What? Oh right. She was supposed to be the ecstatic aunt. Forcing a smile, she said, "I am."

His eyes widened in a look of disbelief.

"I will be," she amended, "when Meg and the baby are at home."

"Ahh." He settled back in his seat, his gaze never leaving her face. "You have a fear of hospitals then."

He said it with such assurance that it was not even a question. She felt her skin warming beneath his gaze. She wasn't used to having her deepest fears on display in front of everyone, but the fact that it was *this* man made it that much worse. She didn't try to deny it, though. It would be ridiculous to try. She was frozen solid in her seat and had been a basket case from the moment the text had arrived.

Of course she was afraid, it must have been written all over her face. And he was a doctor—one who worked at a freakin' hospital. He must see this sort of thing every day.

At that thought, she forced a small smile. "You must deal with this a lot, huh? Patients with an irrational fear of hospitals?"

He reached out and took her ice-cold hand in his. The jolt of awareness as much of a shock as the welcome warmth of his skin against hers.

"But your patients are children," she continued, acutely aware that she was starting to babble. "It makes sense to be afraid if you're a kid."

"Not necessarily," he said. "In my experience, when kids are afraid of hospitals, it's because it's a new environment—one with frightening machines that make weird noises and strangers dressed in strange uniforms, who insist on poking them with sharp objects."

Maggie Dallen

He leaned toward her a bit, and Alice had to resist the urge to meet him halfway so she could lean against his strong warmth.

"But when adults are afraid," he continued slowly, "it's usually because they've had some sort of traumatic experience."

He looked at her then, and she found herself transfixed by his gaze, which seemed to see straight through her. She was naked and vulnerable before him. Of course he saw right through her fears. He wasn't stupid, and he apparently found her appallingly easy to read. She wanted to deny it or make a joke to brush off the oddly intimate moment—but she didn't. She couldn't.

Being here in the hospital, it all came back. The smells and sounds of hospitals always took her right back to that awful, life-changing day. Finding her mother unconscious. The seemingly endless ambulance ride to the hospital. Waiting alone for hours in the waiting room for any word. And finally, that moment when the doctors came to find her.

"My mom died." The words came out softly, but they sounded like a bomb going off in the quiet waiting room. Alice slapped a hand over her mouth in disbelief, but that disbelief turned to horror as tears started to fill her eyes.

It was his fault. He was looking at her with such kindness, such understanding, such love—no, not love. Tenderness, that was what it was. It was impossible not to feel safe, coddled. Like he wanted to ease her pain. And for a stupid, irrational moment, Alice wanted more than anything in the world to let him help. She wanted to tell someone the full story she'd never told anyone else—not even her sister.

Those few years after Meg went off to college and Alice was stuck at home with their erratic, emotional mother and her string of loser boyfriends. Things had gone from bad to worse without Meg's stabilizing influence. Oh, her sister had come home on the weekends to make sure that Alice had meals lined up for the week. To talk to her about her homework and any other teenage issues she might have—but it wasn't the same as when she'd lived there.

But she couldn't tell Meg. She wouldn't add to her sister's already-too-large burden like that. Besides, she'd been old enough at that point to deal with her mother and the dreaded boyfriends on her own. Or so she'd thought.

She'd been wrong.

"How did your mother die?" Nicholas's gentle voice cut through her awful memories, bringing her back to the present, where she realized she was clutching Nicholas's hand like it was a lifeline.

"Drug overdose." There it was. The bitter, harsh truth. She hated saying those words out loud. But Nicholas's eyes didn't hold the pity she expected or the judgment. He remained calm, capable—strong.

"I'm sorry," he murmured.

She shrugged, because that was what she'd always done when people felt sorry for her. She didn't want sympathy. But one tender look from this man dispelled that thought because it wasn't just sympathy in his gaze, it was caring. For some reason she could never explain, he seemed to truly care about her.

Tears were threatening to spill. Godammit, she would not cry in front of this man. Not again.

She took a deep breath, determined to pull herself together. Instead, she found herself talking on the exhale, as if her tears had transformed into a stream of words instead of salty water. Part of her was horrified at the release, but her body seemed to ease as she spoke—the torrent of words needing to escape before she burst from the tension of holding them in.

"She'd always had a problem for as long as I can remember, at least. But she kept it under control, to some extent." Alice stared up at the ceiling, remembering why they were here and battling a surge of fear. "Meg made sure of that." She shook her head, not able to meet Nicholas's eyes, but she could feel them on her, his undiverted attention fixed on her.

"She was always great like that. Meg kept our little house under control. She was the mother that our mom never could be. She made sure our mom ate and stayed hydrated, no matter how bad her binges were. She made sure I was fed and clothed and did my homework." Despite everything, Alice found herself smiling a little at the memory of her older sister's stern motherly ways.

"What changed?" he asked. His voice was undemanding. As if he had all the time in the world to sit here and listen to her sob story.

"Meg left for college. And thank God she did," she hastily added. Looking over to Nicholas, she needed to make it clear. "I was glad she was leaving. So was Mom. Meg was smart, and she deserved a chance at a life. A real life with a real family. We both knew that."

He nodded and Alice felt like he really did understand.

"What happened after she left home?"

Alice heaved a sigh. "She came home on the weekends as often as she could to check in on us, but Mom and I..." She shook her head, trying to sort through the jumbled emotions to find words. "We got good at covering up what was really going on."

Maggie Dallen

The age-old guilt made her chest heavy, which made speaking difficult. She couldn't face Nicholas any longer, not when his kind, understanding gaze was fixed on her as if he could wipe away all the wrongs in her past with a wave of his saintly wand.

"We didn't want her to worry," Alice continued, aware that she was still rationalizing, justifying her own enabling ways during that awful period. "We just wanted her to be happy, you know?"

She thought she heard Nicholas murmur something soothing beside her, but she was too lost in the memories to hear him.

"I should have told Meg what was really going on. I should have told *someone*...."

He waited patiently for her to continue and for a moment she tried not to. She was exposing herself too much. And to a near-stranger. No, not a stranger. But someone she couldn't afford to get close to. Couldn't afford to rely on—not if she wanted to avoid her mother's mistakes.

But something about the quiet intimacy of their surroundings, or maybe it was the late hour and the remnants of the champagne, but Alice found herself completely unable to stop. Getting the words out was a relief after so many years. It was therapeutic. Maybe Meg had been right when she'd urged her to go to counseling all these years.

"There had always been a string of boyfriends," she heard herself say. "My dad left when we were little, and we never saw him again. And after that, there was always someone. They never lasted long, and they were always skeezy creeps."

She felt Nicholas stiffen beside her and heard his unasked question. Shaking her head, she said, "They never took much notice of me and Meg. We were just the annoying brats who happened to hang around the apartment occasionally. The boyfriends usually spent all their time in Mom's bedroom or passed out high on our couch to give us too much trouble."

Until him.

She couldn't continue. She wouldn't. Alice hadn't even told Meg the full truth about Ronnie. She hadn't wanted to make her sister feel any worse than she already had after their mom passed. There was enough guilt to go around between the two of them, and Alice refused to add any more to her sister's plate.

But then Nicholas wrapped an arm around her and pulled her close and the rest of the story spilled out as if he's squeezed the words out of her. "Her last boyfriend came along after Meg left. He wasn't like the others. He noticed."

She shivered slightly at the memory of his leers and crude comments. "I was older then—in high school. I was starting to…develop." "Develop" hardly seemed fit to describe her sudden transformation from gawky tween to curvy woman.

Nicholas was rigid beside her, his arm tight around her shoulders. The reassuring feel of his body pressed against hers made her relax slightly and she let her head fall onto his shoulder. "It wasn't as bad as it could have been," she said. "I managed to avoid Ronnie most of the time. I got really good at finding excuses to stay away from home, to sleep over at friends when I knew he was around. He never touched me…." She shivered with disgust at the memory of one "accidental" hand slip when Ronnie had reached past her for the remote. "Not really, at least."

She let herself soak up some of Nicholas's warmth and his quiet strength before she continued. "But Ronnie was different in another way, too. He was a pusher. He didn't just do drugs with my mom, he got her trying new ones. He was always there with another fix, always egging her on and urging her to do more."

She swallowed back the lump in her throat. "I knew that. I'd seen him in action, but I still stayed away."

She stopped just short of choking on a sob. Biting her lip hard, she waited for it to pass. "Maybe if I hadn't been such a wuss… If I'd stuck around and been there for her…" She couldn't bring herself to finish.

* * * *

Nicholas thought his jaw might shatter from the strength it took not to throw a chair against the wall in rage. He'd seen his share of domestic horror stories working in pediatrics, but he'd never had it be so personal. It had never happened to someone he cared about.

And he did care about her. He couldn't deny it any longer. This was no infatuation or just the thrill of the chase—he cared. He liked her. A lot. And right now she needed him, whether she wanted to or not.

"Alice," he whispered against her hair. "It wasn't your fault."

She nodded, but he knew she didn't believe him. No words from him or anyone else would heal that kind of pain. She needed to talk to someone…a professional. But until then, he would hold her and try to give her whatever it was she needed.

And apparently what she needed was silence. He understood that. Holding her tight, he waited patiently as her breathing slowed and her body relaxed against him. He glanced at the clock. It was going on 1 a.m. They had time—plenty of time. From what Meg's doctor told him it would be many hours yet before Alice became an aunt.

Long nights at a hospital were not new for Nicholas, but he'd never been so happy to be there before. He was content just to sit in silence. Just to feel her against him. He had a feeling this woman didn't lean on many people, and he considered himself lucky that he was one of the chosen few—for tonight, at least.

Nearly an hour passed in companionable silence, each lost in their own thoughts. When Alice did speak, her words were unexpected and seemingly random.

"How do you know Caitlyn?"

Nicholas blinked at the far wall, trying to focus through an exhausted haze. Long nights were a common occurrence—but a long night after an evening of dancing and drinking champagne were a new experience altogether.

Caitlyn. Caitlyn? Then he remembered the brunette from earlier tonight. The sweet woman he'd gone on one date with because she'd sounded like just his type in her profile. It had come as something of a shock to see her here, hugging Alice. But then, he'd learned a long time ago that for a city of eight million, New York was a surprisingly small world.

"We went on a date," he said.

She stiffened beneath his arm. *Interesting.* He wished more than anything that he could see her face but her head was still resting against his chest. Was she…? No, she couldn't be jealous.

"You went on a date?" she echoed.

But then again…could she?

"Mmm." He resisted the urge to explain to her what an abysmal failure that date had been. If she was even a little bit jealous, surely that had to be a good thing. Right?

She shifted against him, as if trying to find a comfortable position. "So what happened?"

He shrugged, knowing she could feel the gesture if not see it. "We weren't as alike as I'd thought we'd be."

She sat up then, turning to him with a scowl. "What do you mean? Caitlyn is the best."

Her defensive tone on her friend's behalf was as sweet as it was disheartening. Maybe she wasn't jealous after all. "She seemed very nice," he said in all honesty. "We just… We didn't want the same things."

She turned to face him for the first time in nearly an hour, and he was struck anew by her beauty. She'd been stunning tonight at the gala, her makeup and dress exquisite, her hair styled perfectly, her curves elegantly highlighted and accentuated without being tacky. The woman was gorgeous, and she knew how to use her looks to her best advantage.

But somehow, tear-stained and rumpled and under the harsh fluorescent lights, he thought she looked more beautiful than ever.

She frowned at him, her brows drawing together as she studied him. "What do you mean?"

He held back a sigh. Why were they talking about Caitlyn? It had been one date—a half hour tops—and nothing had come of it. But she had that relentless look in her eyes so he answered. "I was very specific about what I was looking for in a wife," he started.

Alice's eyes widened instantly, and he inwardly cursed. *Way to go, Hot Doc. You scared her away for good.* He tried to back up and start again, shifting in his seat so he could face her better. He had to get this right or he risked scaring her away forever.

"I've always had a plan," he said. Some of the tension eased out of her shoulders at that. "I'm a big believer in life plans, in setting goals and moving toward them…in every area of my life." God, he sounded like a boring square when he said it out loud.

"And finding a wife was one of those goals?" Alice asked.

To his relief, there was a hint of laughter in her eyes, and she wasn't bolting out the door.

He nodded slowly. "Yes. It makes sense at this point in my life to find a suitable mate."

Her lips were twitching, and he knew exactly how clinical he sounded. He cleared his throat and tried again. "I realize that doesn't sound terribly romantic—"

Alice interrupted using a surprisingly silly robot voice. "This is the appropriate time for a suitable mate."

The unexpected glimpse of this side of her shocked him into a short, loud laugh that seemed to echo off the walls. "All right. Okay. I deserve that."

She was watching him with a small smile, one that was intoxicatingly real.

"My parents were in love." He caught the flicker of surprise at his turn in conversation, but now that the topic had come up, he wanted her to understand. He needed her to get it. "They had this connection." He struggled to come up with a better word for it but failed.

But when he looked at Alice, she was nodding. "That's what Meg has with Jake."

There was something so wistful in her expression that he had to physically resist the urge to pull her into his arms and kiss her senseless.

"That's what I grew up with," he said. "And that's what I hope to find for myself." He left off the next part—the part that would send her running out the door faster than he could say, "Boo!" *I think I already have.*

Maggie Dallen

Her smile grew a bit, and she punched him lightly on the arm. "Now that sounds far more romantic."

He laughed softly. "I suppose it's easier for me to think of everything clinically—in terms of steps and goals and checklists." He met her gaze. "But that doesn't mean there aren't real emotions driving me."

She shifted in her chair, and her eyes darted away as if she was uncomfortable with his sudden seriousness. Or maybe she could sense that he was talking about her—about them.

He refused to ease up. This was his chance to be honest with her—to avoid the games and the teasing and man up. So he leaned forward, his gaze meeting hers once more. "I want a wife. I want a family. But more than that, I want it to be with someone who I have that connection with."

He thought she might look away again, or walk away from him even, but she remained where she was, and her eyes stayed locked on his, though he saw them grow distant as if she was lost in thought. Finally, she nodded decisively. "You deserve that—all of that."

Her unexpectedly kind words were a shock to his system, and he drew back in his chair. It wasn't so much what she said as what she didn't say that brought a stab of pain to his chest. She wasn't saying everyone deserved it. More important, she wasn't saying *she* deserved it, he noticed. And he knew, without her saying anything, that she didn't believe that she deserved that kind of connection or all of the benefits that came with it. Like a family of her own.

He had no idea what he could say that would change her mind. Maybe there was nothing he could do or say—maybe it was something that had to come from her, something she had to realize and accept. No amount of his telling her she was worthy of love would make her believe it—he didn't need to have his doctorate in psychology to know that.

Still, he struggled for words that would help her or that would tell her that he understood, at least.

But before he could think of anything, she was leaning toward him, a fresh excitement making her vibrate with intensity. "You deserve it," she said again. "The family, the connection. All of it."

His heart squeezed painfully in his chest as the meaning behind her words struck him. He hadn't expected her to accept the truth so readily. They couldn't deny their connection. They both deserved to see this through, to see where it might lead—

"I can help you find that," she said.

He was sure his face was comically surprised. *Um... What?*

But she kept going before he could respond. "If you do this bachelor auction, I can help you find someone who you have a connection with. Someone you could have the family with…" Her voice trailed off, and she was watching him expectantly, as if he should be ecstatically cheering that the woman he wanted more than anything in the world was offering to help him find a girlfriend.

Yay?

He bit back the bitter sarcasm. So it was back to this—the stupid bachelor auction.

Frustration had him clenching his jaw as he thought of how best to respond, but a new anger made it difficult to focus. Not only was she trying to sell him off to the highest bidder, but this woman—*his woman*, goddamn it—was now hoping to marry him off to the winner!

There was no way he would passively sit by and let her push him away. Not when he knew, as he did now, what caused it. It wasn't that she didn't like him—there was chemistry between them if nothing else—it was that she didn't think she deserved a real relationship.

Well, like it or not, she was going to get one.

She was still perched on the edge of her seat, her wide sea-green eyes fixed on him, waiting for a response.

"I'll do it," he said. "But you know my conditions."

He heard her inhale sharply. Surely she hadn't forgotten the terms. But then her lips pressed together and her nostrils flared, and he knew without a doubt that she remembered… And she was not pleased that he'd remembered too.

He arched an eyebrow in challenge.

One heartbeat passed, and then another. He found himself holding his breath as he waited for her response.

"Fine," she bit out. "I accept your terms."

Elation shot through him, though he realized how ridiculous that was given the hard tone in her voice.

Way to go, Hot Doc. You just blackmailed the woman you love.

The woman you love… He struggled to inhale as the word struck him like a physical blow to the gut. His mouth fell open, and his eyes widened as shock set in.

He was dimly aware that Alice's eyes had narrowed on him. "Are you all right?"

He tried to form a response but was interrupted when the door to the waiting room flew open and a large man with a grin from ear to ear came in.

"Jake! How is she?" Alice shot out of her seat and ran to hug the man he assumed was her brother-in-law. As they chattered happily and Jake led her back through the double doors, Nicholas sat there frozen in his seat staring after her.

He was too stunned by his own realization to move.

The woman you love... The phrase played on a loop in his brain as he struggled to wrap his head around it. Love. Did he love her? Before he even finished phrasing the question, he knew the answer. Yes. Hell yes. He was in love. With Alice.

Now he just had to make her see that she felt the same way.

Chapter 9

Alice leaned over Ena's shoulder as her friend swiped through the hundreds of baby photos that now filled up all the storage on her phone. She'd flipped through them all herself multiple times—and had seen the little miracle with her own eyes just that morning—but she couldn't seem to get enough.

"She's darling," Ena murmured for the hundredth time, apparently just as smitten as Alice with the newest addition to the family.

The sound of Fred and Ginger singing "Pick Yourself Up" filled the background, adding to Alice's feeling that her heart might burst out of her chest with joy. This was exactly what she'd needed tonight. After returning home from the hospital she'd slept all morning, waking this afternoon feeling…off. That was the only way she could put it.

Oh, she'd still been over the moon about her baby niece and the fact that Meg was healthy and happier than she'd ever seen her, but Alice no longer had the immediate distraction of a baby in her arms, and she could no longer avoid the memories from the night before.

She shut her eyes now as they threatened to return. *Shit, had she really told him all of that?* But spilling her guts wasn't even the worst part—the worst part was that she'd caved. She'd agreed to date him—the man who now knew everything about her. Well, her deepest, darkest secrets, at least.

As if she hadn't already felt naked around that man, now she didn't know what she would do the next time she saw him. He would see straight through her.

"Are you all right?" Ena asked.

Alice's eyes shot open and she quickly forced a smile and a nod. Fine, she was fine, though something deep inside her felt exposed and raw.

But that was one of the reasons she'd found herself at Ena's door tonight. Her friend always stayed up late watching movies, and tonight, Alice hadn't wanted to be alone. She needed someone, which was rare for her, but there it was. She'd needed the quiet comfort of Ena and the black-and-white movies that had always saved her as a kid.

Ena passed back the phone, and the two of them settled back on the couch with their mugs of tea. Alice let her mind go blank as she watched Fred twirl Ginger in his arms in a world where everything was right—where men didn't leave and women didn't ugly cry in hospitals and where happily ever afters were a guaranteed fact.

They hadn't gotten far in the movie when there was a knock at the door, startling Alice. Ena got up and headed to the door as if midnight callers were an everyday occurrence. Alice followed a short distance behind her but froze in mid-step as Ena swung open the door to reveal Nicholas standing there in a pair of faded jeans and a T-shirt, the most casual she'd ever seen him.

And the most handsome.

That was the only thought her brain could conjure before it went blank. She could almost hear her synapses fizzling and dying as a deep-seated fear took root in her gut, leaving her standing there paralyzed.

Nicholas hadn't seen her standing there, and for a moment she watched him interact with Ena like they were old friends. Of course they'd become friends. She'd known that, hadn't she? Ena mentioned that he'd become a daily visitor when she was at the hospital and checked in on his neighbor on a regular basis now that she was home.

He heard Ena's laugh as Nicholas held out a box of "get well" chocolates, as he called them. Then, even though she'd known it was coming, Alice's heart stopped in her chest as Ena opened the door wider and invited him inside.

That was when he saw her. She saw the surprise in his eyes as his gaze met hers. Then there was that soft, kind smile, the one that felt like a warm blanket was being wrapped around her.

"Come on in," Ena was saying. "Alice and I were just watching an old movie. She showed me the pictures of her new niece. Have you seen them?"

He shook his head, following her inside. "I haven't had the chance." To Alice, he added quietly, "Congratulations, by the way. I hear mother and baby are doing great."

She nodded, forcing a polite smile. "They are. Thanks." But he already knew that—he'd probably checked in on them as well, or at least called one of his buddies at the hospital to get their status. Of course he had—that was the kind of guy Nicholas was.

Nicholas followed Ena to the couch, and he took the seat right next to the spot where Alice had been sitting. Ena took her typical spot in the recliner, which left Alice with no option but to sit beside Nicholas.

She half listened as Ena and Nicholas made small talk, and Nicholas asked her some medical questions that went over her head. She should leave, but somehow she was rooted in place, unable to move. Her chest was tight with apprehension, the kind she got before emotional confrontations, when a storm was brewing but she couldn't escape.

After a few minutes, Ena made her excuses, feigning a yawn. "I'm so sorry, you two, but you'll have to watch the rest without me. This medicine makes me tired. I'm heading to bed."

Alice tried to stop her but Ena ignored her pathetic requests to stay up just a little longer. *Don't leave me alone with him!*

But Ena seemed intent on ignoring her. "Alice, you know how to lock up when you leave. You two make yourselves at home and enjoy the movie." She let out another melodramatically loud yawn, and within seconds, the surprisingly spry old lady had shuffled off to her bedroom and shut the door, leaving them alone.

Alice stared after her, absurdly afraid to face Nicholas. When she finally did, he was watching her with concern. "How are you?"

"Fine," she said quickly, automatically.

He studied her in silence for a little while, and she commanded herself not to fidget under his inspection. She knew what he saw and was positive her cheeks were turning red. Why did this man always have to see her at her worst?

She'd never managed to change out of her pajamas today—what was the point when she slept most of the day away? So here she was in a ratty old T-shirt with a beer logo, compliments of Jake's bar, and a baggy pair of sweats that sported a lovely coffee stain. Oh, and then there were the slippers. The fuzzy bunny slippers she'd had since college. Yeah, nothing to be embarrassed about here.

But he didn't mock her attire or even seem to notice how repulsive she was. Instead, he turned his attention to the TV. "So, what are we watching?"

Alice blinked at him in surprise. She'd fully anticipated that Nicholas would expect to talk about the night before, get her to open up again. Once it sank in that he seemed content to just watch a movie with her, she let herself relax back against the couch cushions as she launched into a recap of what had happened up to that point in the movie.

She hadn't really been paying attention to the plot tonight, but she didn't need to. She knew the storyline like the back of her hand. Once he was caught up, they sat in companionable silence for a while watching the musical acts unfold.

After a little while, Nicholas slipped an arm around her shoulder and it seemed like the most natural thing in the world to lean against him. It wasn't until her head fell against his shoulder that she realized she was doing the dreaded…the unexpected…the dangerous. She was cuddling.

What the hell?!

She sat upright quickly, and he straightened in his seat, clearly surprised by the sudden movement. "Everything all right?" he asked.

She nodded, staring straight ahead at the screen. What could she say? *No, you bastard, you had the nerve to cuddle me. And I let you! Everything is not okay.*

Jesus, she would sound like a crazy person. *Get it together, Alice.*

"I'm fine, I just… I just think I should head to bed."

He was so quiet she finally caved and peeked a look in his direction. He was smiling at her—a small, quizzical smile—but one filled with understanding, nonetheless.

"When can I see you again?" he asked.

She swallowed back the panic. Why had she ever agreed to this arrangement?

With a shrug, she tried to change the topic. "We should talk some more about the fundraiser. I have an idea for the venue but if you think—"

He cut her off. "I'm sure whatever you decide will be perfect."

She nodded. That was what she wanted to hear. She liked having control. This was her project, her chance at the promotion. That was why she'd agreed to date this man.

But a flutter of doubt made her uneasy. That *was* the reason she was going along with this, wasn't it?

He got her attention with his next question. "So, about that date... What day works for you?"

When she didn't immediately reply, he asked, "How about tomorrow?"

Alice's mouth was dry but she managed to shake her head. "I can't."

He started to frown, as if he might argue with her, remind her of their deal, most likely. "I can't because I have to help Jake out at the bar. I promised him and Meg that I would help cover for her absence while she's home with the baby."

His expression relaxed. "What time do you think you'll get done?"

She shrugged. "I can probably leave after the happy-hour rush, that's when they really need the help."

His smile was breathtaking. No man should have so much freakin' charm. "Great. I'll pick you up then."

She let out a long breath to try to control her rapid pulse. "So, what are we going to do on our first date?"

His smile altered slightly, one side tugging up higher, giving him a roguish air that was undeniably sexy. "I kind of thought tonight was our first date."

She looked down at her outfit and let out a laugh. "Not much of a first date, is it?"

He shrugged. "I don't know. I'm having a pretty great time. And I couldn't ask for a better date."

The words brought heat rushing to her cheeks. How did he manage to be so sappy yet sound so genuine? The man was unreal. But his words struck a chord, easing some of her tension. The idea that this was a date was oddly reassuring. She'd never done the dating thing before—not the traditional dating thing anyway—and the idea that sitting around watching an old movie counted made her feel slightly more relaxed.

This she could do.

She leaned back against the couch and didn't move away when Nicholas's arm wrapped around her shoulders once more. His touch was warm, reassuring...kind of cozy, really. Slowly but surely she found herself leaning against him, his breath warm on her hair.

One of her favorite musical numbers started, and she tapped his leg with excitement, making him laugh. She was so caught up in the number that she almost forgot that she was nervous and that she was supposed to be keeping her distance.

When it came to an end, his low voice whispered in her ear. "Not bad for a first date, right?"

She looked up at him and smiled. The sharp angles of his face flickered in the shadows caused by the black-and-white screen. He was so handsome. So sane. Such a good guy. What the hell was he doing with someone with as much baggage as her?

She shook off the thought. He was here and so was she, and she had her end of the bargain to live up to. "So this really counts as a date, huh?"

There was that sexy lopsided smile again. "Well, I guess that depends," he said.

"On?"

"Whether you let me kiss you good night."

Everything stopped—or at least, that's how it felt. The sound from the television was drowned out by the sound of her blood rushing in her ears. The only thing she was aware of was the feel of his body pressed against hers, his breath warm against her cheek. The air seemed to thicken around her until it was difficult to breathe.

Her heart picked up its pace as nerves and excitement warred for supremacy.

Her response was way out of proportion to the situation, especially considering she'd already slept with this man. He was just another in a long string of lovers.

But he wasn't, and she couldn't lie to herself that he was. He knew her. And somehow this moment felt a million times more intimate than that night when they'd had sex.

Because now this was no mysterious, handsome stranger. This was Nicholas. Her temporary partner in business and the man who had somehow cracked through all of her defenses. He'd seen the worst of her, and he hadn't run away.

Maybe that was why she didn't try to stop him as he leaned in toward her. She couldn't. At some point over the past few weeks, this man had broken down all her defenses and she was powerless. Weak. Normally that would have terrified her, but right now, that terror was overshadowed by the need to feel his lips on hers again. The need to feel that connection at a deeper level.

His kiss didn't disappoint. His lips against hers were tender—gentle but strong as he wrapped his arms around her until she was in a cocoon, fully protected from the world around her by the safe, secure haven of his arms.

The kiss erased any remaining doubts or terror. Her mind was blissfully blank as his lips urged hers apart and his tongue teased hers, slipping inside to tangle with hers in a soft, lingering kiss that turned her body to liquid heat.

When he finally pulled his head up for air, she found herself sighing against his lips, her eyes firmly shut. She didn't want it to end.

He leaned back in and placed one more light but searing kiss against her lips. "Good night, sweetheart."

She didn't open her eyes even as she heard him get up from the couch and head toward the door. She didn't want the moment to end and she held on to the blissful feeling until she fell asleep on Ena's couch.

* * * *

Alice made one stop on her way to work at Jake's after leaving the office a little early.

"Hey, Alice," Tamara called out as she entered The Ellen's lobby. "How's Meg?"

"She's great. She and baby Isabelle are at home and doing well." She moved to follow Tamara, who was heading toward the tiny office just off the lobby. "I actually came to see you about something else though...."

Tamara stopped and turned, her brows raised in a questioning look. "What's up?"

Alice launched into her spiel, explaining about the fundraiser that was scheduled for three weeks' time and her need for a new venue. One with character, one that was unique, one suited for a performance, of sorts....

"Like The Ellen?" Tamara guessed with a teasing smile.

"Exactly like The Ellen." Alice rested her hip against the desk in the office and watched Tamara sink into the seat, which looked way too large for her tiny frame. She looked almost like a child with her big blue eyes and long fair hair. "What do you think? I haven't met the new owner yet... Do you think he'd go for it?"

To Alice's surprise, Tamara turned a pretty shade of pink at the mention of the new owner. The deal had only been finalized the week before, and all Alice really knew about him was what they all knew from the papers— Gregory Blanchard was a legendary real estate mogul and heir to old money. He was also best friends with Ben, and Caitlyn swore he was a great guy, with only the best intentions for the old theater.

Still, her friend's reaction to his name was interesting. She was tempted to think her friend had a crush if she didn't know Tamara so well. Tamara had a major aversion to dating and seemed completely immune to men in general. Though maybe not gorgeous billionaires who were consistently named bachelor of the year, it seemed....

Tamara regained her composure quickly. "I think he'd go for it. He's really into the idea of turning The Ellen into an event space to help offset the cost of running it as a solely classic film theater."

Alice beamed. "So you'll talk to him?"

Tamara only hesitated for a second, but Alice caught it. "Sure, I'll talk to him about it."

Alice planted a kiss on her friend's cheek. "You are the best, Tam. Thank you!"

* * * *

She saw Tamara again a few hours later, along with Marc and Caitlyn, who had all stopped by the bar to congratulate Jake once again and to see the latest pictures of Baby Isabelle. Caitlyn had seen the new mom and baby that morning, so she had the latest pictures for everyone to coo over.

Between hanging out with her friends and helping to work the busy bar, Alice had thought that maybe she wouldn't have time to be nervous about the date to come.

She was wrong. All day she'd been battling with the butterflies in her stomach, but now, as the clock inched toward seven o'clock and she knew it was just a matter of time before he arrived—Alice was a ball of nerves.

When he showed up, looking like he'd just stepped off a runway in his leather jacket and nicely fitted jeans, the nerves dissipated somewhat. It was his smile that did it—when had that smile become such a calming influence? When had he become such a steadying force that his mere presence made her anxiety decrease and her heart swell with something close to contentment?

She raised a finger in the "one minute" gesture as she finished clearing off a dirty table. She watched from across the bar as he greeted her friends, who seemed to include him into their little group like he was a long-lost member of their tribe.

She tried not to be jealous when Caitlyn said something that made him laugh, but it was impossible to stop the rush of possessiveness. But it wasn't just jealousy, it was something worse. Seeing Caitlyn and him sitting together was a vivid reminder of just how ill-suited she was for him.

She knew that—she'd always known that. It was what she'd been trying to tell him all along. But seeing it was a bitter reminder. He deserved someone just like Caitlyn. Not her, of course, since she was madly in love with her boyfriend. But someone like her—someone sweet and kind and uncomplicated. Someone who believed in true love and marriage and families.

Not that Alice didn't love the idea of marriage and kids—she fully supported the institution…for those who were suited to it. But it was not for people like her. There were some parts of her that were just too broken to fix.

Nicholas glanced in her direction, and she saw his brow furrow with concern at whatever he saw in her expression, so she forced herself to let go of the dark thoughts and smile in his direction. He returned the smile, but she still saw concern in his eyes.

When she was finally done, she stepped up to him, absurdly nervous. This was ridiculous. She was a grown woman, not a teenager. This was hardly her first date.

Although, it kind of was.

It was the first real date, at least. The first where she wasn't 100 percent in control, and where the end objective wasn't to end up in bed with her date. She looked up at the profile of his chiseled jaw as he led the way out of the bar and flashed back on the way he'd kissed every part of her body that night when they'd made love. Yeah, maybe that wouldn't be the worst conclusion to this date.

He glanced down at her, and one side of his lips curled up. "What's so funny?"

She shook her head. "Nothing." It wasn't until they were a block away that she thought to ask, "So, where are you taking me tonight?"

He reached down and his hand clasped hers. The warmth of his hand around hers felt good...safe. But the gesture was oddly intimate and she resisted the urge to jerk her hand away. She shook her head at her own stupidity. If she was going to make it through this whole dating thing with her heart intact, she was going to have to man up. A simple hand hold was not going to kill her.

But her mind was stuck on the realization that she was worried about her heart. Holy shit, when had her heart become at stake? At what point had she become so vulnerable to this man?

From that very first night, she supposed. He'd cracked through her defenses on that first night and had only managed to wheedle himself in farther ever since. So yes, her heart was at risk here.

Was that really so bad?

Yes! Of course it was. She didn't want to lose her heart—to anyone. Wasn't that what she'd learned from her mother? Wasn't that the promise she'd made to herself all those years ago?

His voice called her back to the present as he laid out his plan for the evening, starting with drinks at a bar a few blocks away. "Then I was thinking we could go to my friend Claudia's for dinner."

He looked down at her, and she nearly melted at the warm intimacy in his gaze. He was looking at her like she was his date, she realized. More than that—like she was his girlfriend, maybe. He was looking at her...like he cared.

Her heart squeezed in her chest painfully. Dammit, she liked that look.

"If that's okay with you," he added. "Claudia loves to throw dinner parties, and I know she really enjoyed talking with you at the gala and—"

"That sounds great," Alice interrupted. And it did. Dinner at Claudia's meant other people would be around, and a crowd was exactly what she needed to keep some distance, get some perspective.

She was rewarded with a smile and a hand squeeze before he tugged her toward a cozy pub that was down a long flight of stairs. The bar was warm, with candles dotting every surface and a warm buzz of conversation filling the air, along with soft jazz music.

He led her toward a small table in the back that had been reserved for them. When they were seated across from one another, Alice nearly caved to the romantic atmosphere. He was gazing at her in the candlelight, and it was all so…intimate. The effect made her heart hurt as the same time as an age-old panic started to set in.

It was the same flight or fight response that always seemed to happen when intimacy threatened—but especially with this man. It was like her body had known from the very beginning that this man was trouble. He was dangerous because he had the power to hurt her.

Reaching across the table, he grasped her hand in his and stroked his thumb over the pulse at her wrist. "Are you all right?"

She nodded, but her voice was tight. "What are you doing here with me, Nicholas?"

His brows drew together, and his eyes filled with concern. "What do you mean? We're on a date—"

She shook her head. "I mean why do you want to be with me? I've done nothing but push you away."

He looked like he was going to answer, but she didn't want to hear it. That wasn't true, she did want to hear it. She wanted to be reassured. But that need was ridiculous, she was supposed to be keeping her distance, his reasons shouldn't matter. So she found herself saying, "You should be here with someone like Caitlyn."

The moment the words left her mouth, she knew she'd hurt him. Her stomach churned as she saw the flicker of pain in his eyes—but it was there and gone in an instant. "Maybe," he said. "But I'm here with you."

So even he could admit that he should be with someone else. "Why? Why are you fighting so hard for a date with me?"

He looked thoughtful for a moment, his eyes studying her face as if he could read everything about her there. And maybe he could—he seemed to be able to see her in a way that no one else could.

"You're not the easiest person to get to know," he said, startling her into a short laugh at his candor. Her laugh died instantly as he continued. "But maybe that's part of the reason I like you so much."

She blinked at him in the candlelight, the words wrapping around her like a warm blanket despite her efforts to push them away.

"You're not the kind of woman I was looking for." His hand squeezed hers as if to ease the sting of the words, but she wasn't hurt. They were the truth, and they made sense.

"So what are you doing here with me?" The words came out as a whisper, and she forced herself to talk a little louder, with a confidence she no longer felt. "You should be with someone sweet, someone easy, someone who wants the same things that you do."

There was a brief silence, and Alice watched his slow smile form as if hypnotized by the curve of his lips. "First of all, sweet is not necessarily the same thing as kind. And you are kind, Alice, whether you choose to admit it or not."

His words made her stiffen. No one had ever called her that—oh, Meg maybe, but never a man.

"I've seen you with Ena, when you talk about your sister and your friends. Yes, you are prickly and self-contained, but beneath that there is a huge heart just waiting to love someone."

Alice opened her mouth to deny it. She was not looking for love. How many times had she told herself that? How many times had she said it to others? But here, now, when it really counted, she couldn't get the words out.

She finally managed to say, "Your life would be easier with someone else. Anyone else." Because that was the truth. She had more than her share of baggage and life with her would never be easy.

When had she started to contemplate a life with this man? With any man?

"Probably," he said matter-of-factly, shocking her back to the moment at hand. She found herself laughing softly at his honesty—at least he wasn't trying to deny that she was difficult.

He leaned over the table, his grip on her hand tightening. "Maybe my life would be easier if I'd fallen for someone else. But I like you. I choose to be with you, any day of the week."

Her breath hitched in her throat, and her heart stopped beating entirely before it sped up so quickly she thought she might faint. *If I'd fallen for someone else.* He was dangerously close to admitting true feelings for her. The L-word. Something too deep and scary for her to contemplate. She focused on his other words and they rang in her ears. *I choose to be with you.*... Despite herself, the words affected her. They were heady, intoxicating. She tried to fight their effect, but it was too late. They'd taken root in her chest—deep down where her darkest insecurities lie. *He chose her.* This man with his kind eyes and perfect smile—this man with his stable, normal upbringing and his clear-headed view of life—somehow he found her good enough, damaged as she was.

Disbelief warred with a surprisingly intense desire to believe it. She shouldn't. She should be fighting this, fighting him. But she could feel her defenses weakening as a long-forgotten part of her heart clung to his words, wanting to believe them.

She forced herself to argue, but it was a half-hearted attempt. "Your life would be easier if you liked someone else."

He shrugged. "Easy is overrated."

"You deserve to be with someone—"

"Who challenges me," he finished smoothly. "Who makes feel passion—something that has been largely lacking in my life."

She thought about laughing off his words—skewing them to be about sex alone, make it about something cheap and meaningless, but the sincerity in his eyes wouldn't let her. She knew he wasn't talking about physical passion—or at least, not just that.

"Up until you, my life has been focused on goals and achievements," he said. "With you, all that falls to the side. All those goals mean nothing if I don't have someone to share them with."

She stared into his eyes, trying to find any flicker of doubt, but there was none. His honesty overwhelmed her. His ability to expose himself like that made her feel weak in comparison. When was the last time she'd been so brutally honest with another person? Other than her sister, she'd never said the words "I love you" to a single soul. She'd never admitted to anyone that she needed them—not even Meg.

She didn't know what to say in response. Even if she could make sense of the swelling tide of emotions that was threatening to drown her, she wouldn't know how to begin to put them into words.

But he didn't seem to mind her silence. He gave her that warm smile, squeezed her hand, and beckoned for their waiter to order a glass of wine.

The next hour passed in pleasant conversation about everything under the sun, though they both steered clear of the fundraiser topic as if by unspoken agreement. After they finished their drink, Nicholas paid and led her outside to catch a cab uptown to Claudia's apartment.

They could hear the low murmur of voices from the hallway—a pleasant, homey sound of people laughing and talking. Unexpected nerves rose up but Alice tried to steel herself against them.

She was already feeling exposed and raw after their conversation earlier, and her normal social façade—the one she hid behind to keep from having genuine conversations—felt broken and ill-fitting.

Claudia greeted them with a grin, pulling Alice into a hug, which eased some of the tension. She could do this. It was one evening with pleasant strangers—nothing to fear.

When she got home tonight—alone, she promised herself—then she could weed through the emotions that were coming up, begging to be addressed. But for now, she wouldn't notice them. She would smile and laugh and do her damnedest to get through the rest of the night without dwelling on their conversation.

Nicholas stayed by her side all evening, for which she was grateful. Even with her pep talk, she didn't feel quite as capable of making small talk as she normally would—her brain had a bad habit of drifting back to their earlier conversation, replaying bits and pieces in its attempt to process it all.

Which was probably why she wasn't paying attention when the topic of Nicholas's potential promotion first came up after dinner as they sipped on their wine in the living room.

Nicholas must have tried to wave away a compliment, because Claudia's voice boomed out in the room, bringing Alice back to the present. "Are you kidding me?" Claudia said as she topped off another guest's glass. "Nicholas is a shoo-in for the position. He's worked his ass off to get where he is, and the board knows it."

Claudia glanced her way as if looking for a partner to back her up on this—to say, "Hell yeah, Nicholas deserves this more than anyone!" but Alice couldn't quite do it. She was too busy realizing that she had no idea what promotion they were talking about—after all the listening Nicholas had done, all the interest he'd taken in her and her life, how selfish was she that she hadn't bothered to ask him about his career goals?

She opened her mouth to ask Nicholas for the details—he was sitting beside her, one arm brushing against hers as they sank into the couch cushions. But before she could, one of the other guests—a nurse from the hospital—interjected. "I don't know why you're so excited about this promotion, Claudia. You're going to miss him more than anyone if he heads off to Boston."

Alice froze with her mouth slightly parted, still facing Nicholas, but the question died on her lips. Her brain registered the words, but the crushing pain in her chest sidelined her. He was leaving.

He was leaving her.

No one else in the room seemed to notice that her world had just been flipped upside down, her heart crushed—which was ridiculous since they weren't even a couple. Not really. His actions shouldn't have this much power over her.

Try telling that to the searing pain in your chest.

She heard Claudia's response, saying how she would support Nicholas wherever he went, how he deserved this promotion.

Maybe that's how she should have felt too—he was starting to be a friend, at the very least. Maybe she should be feeling supportive. But all she could focus on was the sharp, bitter betrayal of it all. Why hadn't he told her he was leaving?

If he knew he was leaving, why the hell had he pursued her? Why had he made her care?

But then, his reasons did matter. Despite his sweet words and earnest actions, he'd always known he was going to leave. Just like they all did.

She swallowed down a wave of nausea. After all these years of trying to avoid her mother's curse, she'd gone and done the unthinkable. She'd fallen for a guy just to watch him walk away. Like a fool, she'd let him in, and now she would pay the price.

She turned to face the others, steeling her expression and hoping that her rage wasn't as obvious as it felt—because it felt like her blood was boiling and steam was about to come shooting out of her ears.

When there was a lull in the conversation, she turned to Nicholas. "I'm getting tired. I think I need to call it a night."

His eyes widened in surprise, but he nodded quickly. "Yes, of course. I'll go get our coats."

Claudia followed Alice as she dropped off her wine glass next to the kitchen sink. *Go away*, she wanted to shout at the other woman. *I need to get out of here without any more talking.* Because if she opened her mouth to talk, she had no idea what might come out. Tears or screams of rage. Either way, she needed to run before she exploded.

But Claudia didn't seem to hear her internal plea for space. She came up and gave Alice a hug. "I'm so glad you could come tonight. It means the world to me and Frank to see Nicholas so happy."

Those words were shards of glass. So happy. Because he'd made a conquest of her? Clearly that was all he'd wanted because he'd failed to tell her that this was only temporary. That he was leaving—*like they all did.*

A little voice in her brain shouted that she was being a hypocrite. A melodramatic hypocrite, at that. You never wanted this to be permanent. You'd made that clear.

She never even wanted to date him in the first place. He was the one who'd pushed for this, not her. She would have been happy with one night. *Liar.*

Well, she wouldn't have been hurt, at least.

Claudia pulled back and gave her a searching look. "Are you all right?"

She forced a nod and a smile. *My heart is being shredded into a million pieces as we speak, but don't worry, I'll be just fine. I always am.*

Claudia's smile was warm and understanding. "New relationships are hard," she said softly. "They're scary."

Alice's smile froze on her face. Is that what Claudia thought this was? Is that what he'd told her?

She was disgusted by the way her heart responded, as if the clouds had just parted and it had seen sunshine for the first time. Stupid, ridiculous emotions. He's not staying. He hadn't even tried to deny it when the others took it for granted that he'd be leaving. *So what if Claudia thinks this is for real—you know better.*

"The good news is Nicholas is one of the good ones," Claudia said, squeezing her arms in a reassuring gesture. "You can trust him."

I did trust him, that's the problem. Tears threatened to choke her, but she forced herself to nod. It wasn't this woman's fault that Nicholas was just like every other man—selfish and set to run. She was just being a loyal best friend, which Alice couldn't fault.

No, the only person at fault here was her. She'd gone and trusted him. A veritable stranger and a guy who wanted to sleep with her. Oh, she was so stupid. So incredibly dumb. For all her big talk of her three-date-rules and her no-guys-allowed in her private space policies…she'd gone and let one in. And not just any one—the most dangerous of them all. Because he'd thoroughly fooled her with his kind smile and gentle eyes. He'd tricked her into thinking he was different.

"You all set?" Nicholas's low voice behind her gave her a start. Still not trusting herself to speak, she gave Claudia one last smile of thanks and made a beeline for the door.

Chapter 10

Something was wrong with Alice—he'd known it for the last twenty minutes but hadn't known how to get her alone to see what the problem was. But now they were alone on the sidewalk, and she was stalking away from him toward the avenue at the end of the block where cabs were whizzing past.

He hurried after her. "Alice, wait up." But she never stopped moving, not until he reached her side and placed a hand on her arm. Then she whirled around to face him, and the sheer pain and anger written in her expression were like a punch in the gut. The air rushed from his lungs at the sight.

"Alice, what's wrong?"

Her lips pressed together, and he saw her hands clench at her sides she stared at him. Finally, she bit out, "You're leaving."

He was stunned by the depth of emotion in her voice—so floored by the rawness of her reaction that it took a moment for the words to register. Leaving? Then the pieces clicked into place. The promotion, the potential move that would entail. He shook his head. "No, not yet. I mean nothing has been decided. I may not even—"

"You'll get it." It should have been a compliment, but her words were bitter, twisted. "You'll get the promotion, everyone knows that because that's the way things work out for you, isn't it?"

Yes. She was right, and he knew it. Everything had come easily in his life—oh, he'd worked hard for his success, but when it really mattered, he'd always gotten his way. It was a result of good planning, hard work.... That was what he'd always told himself. But now none of that hard work or planning seemed to matter because the only thing he cared about at that moment was Alice—and she was glaring at him with something frighteningly close to disgust.

"You get everything you want," she sneered. "The Prince Charming doctor with his charming smile and his loving family and the adoring women..."

Her words struck him with a physical force, shards of glass that ripped through the perfect life he'd built for himself. What did any of it matter if he didn't have her?

"I knew from the very beginning that I shouldn't trust you."

"What? Alice, no. Why would you think that?"

But she wasn't listening. She was lost in her own pain, and there was nothing he could do to stop it. He could see the misery in her eyes, the betrayal.

"You made me think I could trust you." His heart stopped at the choked sob in her voice. Shit, had he done this? But he hadn't meant to hurt her.

"You made me think you were different." She shook her head. "God, I am such an idiot."

"Alice, no. Let me explain."

She turned tear-filled eyes up to him, her face contorted in pain. "Why did you make me like you? Why couldn't you just leave me alone?"

Despite the agony of seeing her in pain, a spark of hope had him reaching out toward her. She liked him, she admitted it. He could save this, make her see.

"Alice, I didn't tell you because it didn't seem important."

She raised her brows and let out a cynical laugh. "You didn't tell me because you didn't care. You were only focused on one thing—getting the woman you couldn't have. I was a challenge, an interesting phenomenon. A side-step on your great life plan, but not a part of it."

He blinked at her as her words registered. The worst part was that there was some truth to it. Not that he'd only been chasing her for the challenge, he'd long since figured out that she was so much more to him than just the thrill of the chase. She was Alice. She was his. She was everything.

But he hadn't thought ahead. For the first time in his life he'd been acting on sheer impulse and emotion and had left planning and logic in the dust. How had he imagined this working out? He couldn't say. He hadn't been thinking beyond the present moment. "You're right," he said. Before she could respond, he hurried on. "Not about all of it, but about me not factoring you into my life plans. I didn't, but not because you're not important to me...."

He watched her jaw clench and he knew she was fighting back tears. Dammit, why couldn't he think of the words to make her see?

"You weren't part of the plan," he said. "But that's what I love about you."

Her head snapped back at his use of the word "love" and he hurried on. "You took me by surprise. You shook up everything in my world, and you turned it upside down."

Her brows drew together, and he knew he was getting through to her. She was listening, at least, and that was a start.

"The promotion isn't a certainty, but even if I do get it…" He paused as the truth of what he was about to say shook him to his core. "If you want me to stay, I'll stay."

Her eyes widened, mirroring the shock he felt himself. It was almost dizzying, the sudden and complete shift his brain had just made thanks to the shove from his heart. For the first time in his life, he was going off script. He would derail his great plans, happily, if it meant that she was a part of his life.

"You don't mean that," she whispered. He could hear the uncertainty in her voice, the desire to believe him—it was faint, but it was there and it gave him hope.

He moved a little closer so he could feel the heat from her body, the warm assurance that she was here, with him, where she belonged. "I do mean it." He shook his head in frustration. "Look, Alice, you may not have been part of the plan, but screw the plan."

She was starting to shut him out, he could see it as clear as day in the way her posture stiffened and her eyes grew shuttered. She was retreating, and it frustrated the hell out of him. He was putting himself out there— he was offering to derail his career plans for her, and she was shutting him out. Again.

He couldn't disguise the anger in his voice as sheer frustration took hold. "Alice, I care about you. I've made that clear from the start—just like you've made it clear that you don't want me."

She stiffened at that—but it was the truth, and she knew it.

"Tell me you want me to stay and I'll stay. Let me in, Alice, and I'm yours. We'll make decisions together. Hell, we'll create a new plan—for the two of us." He'd hoped to lighten the mood with that, maybe see an inkling of a smile, but he was losing her. He could see her emotional retreat just as surely as if she'd took off in a dead run.

"You don't mean that," she said again but louder this time. There was no doubt in her voice. She wasn't looking to be contradicted. She was assuring herself that she was right not to trust him in the first place.

Desperation had him plowing ahead, even though he knew his words weren't registering through that thick wall of defenses she'd built around her. Still, he had to say it. He was losing her, and he couldn't have that. Not without a fight. Not without laying it all out on the line. "As important as my career is…I love you more."

The silence that fell between them was so thick he thought he might scream just to shatter it. There it was. The sacred words he'd never said to another woman. He was nearly as shocked as she looked, but he felt the rightness of them. He'd known it for ages, possibly from the first moment they'd met. Love at first sight was a cliché he'd never believed in until he'd felt it.

But none of that mattered if she didn't feel the same way. Any hope that he'd been harboring withered and died as he watched her expression shift from surprise to something else, something hard and unreadable.

Alice turned then, not giving him a second look as she stalked off toward the avenue leaving his words hanging out there in the cold, her arms wrapped around herself as if she was in physical pain.

He didn't go after her. He couldn't. His chest was ripping open, his heart tearing in two. So this was it. This was love. Claudia had been right—it was not convenient, it was messy, and it doesn't fit into any of the well-planned boxes in life.

It also hurt like hell.

* * * *

He stumbled back to Claudia's to nurse the pain. Luckily the other guests had left shortly after he and Alice so he was free to sprawl across her couch and let Claudia and Frank stare at him with pity. He couldn't bring himself to care how pathetic he looked.

Claudia handed him another drink—one he definitely didn't need. "So let's get this straight," she said with a forced lightness. "This was your first official date…. And you told her you loved her."

He groaned as he threw an arm over his face. "I'm an idiot."

"No," Claudia said quickly. "I'm not mocking. It was a gutsy move."

"Very brave," Frank added, raising a glass as if to toast the courageous imbecile.

What had he been thinking? Nothing could scare her away faster than talk of love. He didn't have to be a psychologist to figure that out. But as much as his words haunted him, he couldn't bring himself to regret it. At least he'd said his piece. If he never saw her again, at least he knew that he'd put it all out there. That he'd tried.

He shut his eyes as another wave of misery washed over him. What did trying matter if he lost her for good?

He turned to look at Claudia—wonderful, competent, emotionally intelligent Claudia. She always knew what to do, and there was nothing she loved more than giving advice.

"What now?" he asked.

Claudia stared at him blankly. "What do you mean, what now?"

He shifted so he was sitting upright. "What do I do now? How do I make her see that we should be together?"

Claudia and Frank exchanged a look that had some of his newfound hopefulness fading as quickly as it came about. Then they both turned to him with pity in their eyes, and the remainder of his hope faltered and died.

"I don't know that there's anything you can do," Claudia said. "You told her you love her. You've told her you'd give up this promotion for her, if she asked it…. I don't think there's anything more you can say or do at this point."

He stared at his friend in shock. This was not the Claudia advice he was looking for. "So what—you two think I should give up?"

"Not give up," Frank said quickly. He and Claudia exchanged another one of those couple looks where they seemed to be communicating telepathically.

"I just think this is up to her now," Claudia said. "She needs to figure out if she can trust you."

If she loves you… That was the unspoken part she left off.

She was right and he knew it, but it still sucked. It was out of his hands. He took a sip of his scotch and stared into its amber depths. No amount of strategizing or planning could help him now.

He'd never felt so useless.

Chapter 11

Alice found herself on Meg's doorstep. It was late but she had a key and she hadn't been able to bring herself to go home to her empty studio. She just couldn't do it. Using her spare key, she slipped into their downtown apartment. She didn't want to wake Meg, she just couldn't stand the thought of being alone. Not tonight.

"Welcome home, Sis," she heard Meg's voice say from the darkness of the living room before a light switched on.

Meg was in a rocking chair feeding the baby, and she was smiling until she took one look at Alice's tear-stained face. "Oh, honey, what happened?"

One hour and two cups of tea later, Alice had told her sister everything. The baby had long since fallen back to sleep, and guilt gnawed at Alice. "You should get some sleep too," she said. "You're going to be exhausted in the morning."

Meg waved off her concern. "I'll be exhausted in the morning no matter what. It's called being a new mom. Besides, I'm your big sis first and foremost."

Alice felt tears welling up once again— God, she was so sick of crying. But Meg had always been so much more than just a big sister—she was mother, father, and sister all in one. And right now she was channeling the mother role in a big way.

"What is this really about?" she asked, her arms folded over her chest.

"He lied to me."

Meg tilted her head as she considered that. "Not really. He just didn't tell you about a possible promotion."

"That would make him move." Alice stuck her lower lip out and realized belatedly what a stubborn child she must look like. "He should have told me."

"When?" Meg asked.

Alice's head shot up. "What do you mean when?"

Meg arched one brow. "I mean when do you think he should have discussed this with you—when you were kicking him out of your apartment? When you were rejecting his phone calls and turning down his requests for a date?"

Alice scowled at her sister. Why was she on the defensive here? Still, some of her sister's logic was starting to sink in, and she hated the growing pit of unease that told her maybe she wasn't totally in the right—and maybe he wasn't completely in the wrong.

She had been pushing him away. But she'd been right to… Hadn't she?

"He's just going to leave. He would have left no matter what."

Meg stared at her. "That is the most cynical thing I've ever heard."

Alice rolled her eyes. How her sister turned out to be such a romantic was a mystery. They'd grown up in the same household, after all, seen the same disastrous conclusions to every new "romance" that came up. It was all giggles and smiles in the beginning but sobbing and binges in the end.

No, thanks.

She sniffed and avoided her sister's watchful stare. It was for the best. Sure it hurt now, because she'd stupidly let herself get close—but better to get hurt now than to be crushed by him later after she'd well and truly lost her heart.

Too late. A fresh round of tears started to well up and she clamped her lips together to hold them in.

She heard Meg sigh beside her. As usual, her sister seemed to be reading her mind. "Oh, honey…. You're in love, aren't you?"

"No!" *Yes.* An inner voice mocked her instant and vehement denial. "Maybe." She could feel Meg's eyes on hers and didn't want to see the pity there. She focused on toying with the edges of a baby blanket on her lap. "I don't know, okay?"

How was she supposed to know what it was that she was feeling when it was nothing she'd ever felt before? She'd thought she was immune to love—she'd done everything in her power to keep it at bay, to ward it off. But whatever it was she was feeling for Nicholas, it was strong and overwhelming, and it made her heart feel like it might burst out of her chest.

Just thinking of the way he'd looked at her when he'd said those words that were too good to be true, *As important as my career is… I love you more.* The L-word echoed in her ears, mocking her, taunting her. It was a gauntlet thrown down, a challenge to her—to her heart and her willpower and to everything she'd trained herself to believe for the last twenty years.

Meg wrapped an arm around her shoulders, and after a moment of resistance, she let herself be pulled in for an embrace. The hug shattered the last of her self-control and the tears she'd been battling came out in a gut-wrenching sob that tore her heart in two.

"I don't know what to do," she choked out through her tears.

"What's the problem, Alice? He loves you, and it's pretty obvious that you care about him as well."

She hesitated only briefly before nodding. Yes, she could admit that she cared about him. He was kind and gentle, and he'd worked his way past her defenses. Of course she cared, she wasn't heartless.

"So what's the problem?" Meg asked again.

Alice took a deep bracing breath, trying to stifle the sobs. If there was anyone who could understand, it would be her sister. "I don't want to be like *her.*"

By Meg's sigh, Alice knew her sister understood.

"You're nothing like her." Meg's tone was so sharp, so insistent, Alice drew back in surprise. She moved so she could see her sister's face and was shocked anew at the ferocity she saw there.

"Mom was scared of everything," Meg said. "She couldn't handle challenges, couldn't be on her own." Meg sighed again, and the exhale held a world of sadness. "Mom, God bless her… She wouldn't have known true love if it smacked her in the face."

Alice blinked at her sister in surprise. They'd never talked about their mother like this. After her death, they'd only ever focused on the good, as if by some unspoken rule. So to hear Meg criticize her was like opening a door that had been long sealed.

"Why not?" Alice asked. "She thought she was in love...so many times."

Meg's face softened, her eyes filled with pity at the memory of their mother and her pathetic dependency on men. "I figured out a long time ago that she never truly loved those men. She couldn't have because our mother was too afraid to fall in love."

Alice frowned at her sister as the words registered. She couldn't deny that their mother lacked in the courage department. Everything from her choice in men to her dependency on drugs spoke of a deep-seated weakness. An inability to face life. But afraid to fall in love? It was what their mother did best… She was forever in a state of falling for one loser or another.

Meg brushed Alice's hair out of her face like she had when they were kids. "You know what I learned when I fell in love with Jake? That falling in love...real love...is scary. Quite possibly the scariest thing that's ever happened to me. I think it's even scarier for us, in particular, because we've seen what bad relationships look like up close and personal."

Alice met her sister's eyes. She knew what her sister was getting at, and she finished for her. "But those relationships weren't real love."

Meg shook her head vehemently. "No. They weren't. You know why? Because to really love you have to trust. And trusting is another person is scary, especially for the women in the Klein household, because we were never shown how it was done."

Trust. The word was like an accusation in and of itself. She'd only ever truly trusted one person in this world, and she was sitting right beside her.

"You can't have love without trust," Meg continued. "But it works both ways, you know. He has to trust you too. He's trusting you not to break his heart."

Let me in, Alice, and I'm yours. Alice slapped a hand over her mouth to keep from sobbing out loud. Had he meant it? Had he meant it when he'd said he loved her? Only she could decide that, but it would require trust. She would have to have faith that he was being honest with her. And if he was?

Then he loved her. He'd put his heart in her hands. And she had the power to break it. The thought was humbling. If he'd truly meant it... Then she'd just walked away, and left him there. Alone. Now it was guilt that had her chest tightening with a fresh wave of tears.

"I don't want to hurt him," she said.

Meg tilted her head to the side. "What makes you think you would?"

She looked at her sister with one brow raised in disbelief. "Are you kidding? I don't know the first thing about being in a relationship...about being in love." The word was even hard to say out loud. "What if I'm not capable of love?" *Like her?*

Meg met her gaze with a level look. "You're nothing like her, Alice. You are strong, you always have been. The only way you could end up like her is if you cave in to your fears and run away from genuine emotions."

That was exactly what she'd been doing ever since their mother's death, and they both knew it. She'd been gliding along pretending that casual sex was a good enough substitute for a real relationship, keeping their friends at arm's length, keeping the world at arm's length.

"Pushing love away," Meg said slowly, "it might keep you safe from having your heart broken, but it's no way to live. That's not life."

Alice drew in a deep breath and let her head fall against her sister's shoulder. "It didn't work."

"What?"

She almost laughed at the patheticness of it all. "I tried so hard to keep my heart safe by not falling in love but...it happened anyway." He'd slipped through her armor somehow, and whether she wanted to admit it or not, he'd gotten to her. He'd made her fall in love.

Meg's shoulder moved beneath her head, and Alice realized her sister was laughing softly. "Yeah, love has a tendency to hit you when you least expect it."

Alice found herself smiling despite herself. "So you're saying I got struck with a case of stealthy ninja love?"

Meg laughed out loud at that. "Exactly."

Alice sighed and for a moment they sat there in silence, lost in thought.

"Hey, you want to see if there's an old musical on TV?" Meg asked.

Alice smiled but she could hear the exhaustion in her sister's voice. "Nah, you get some sleep while you can. Besides, much as I'd love to escape, I think it's about time I face the real world."

Her sister gave her a hug before heading off to bed, leaving Alice alone with her racing thoughts and a heart that refused to be ignored.

* * * *

The next morning was an Operation Petticoat morning. Alice had planned to skip it the night before, but after a night of sleepless tossing and turning on Meg's pullout couch, she was stir-crazy and itching to get out.

Maybe a little manual labor was exactly what she needed.

It was a mistake. From the moment she walked through the door her friends seemed to know just how messed up she was. Maybe they could tell she'd spent the night crying thanks to her puffy eyes, or maybe it was the fact that she couldn't manage to summon up a smile for the life of her.

It was just Caitlyn, Tamara, and Marc that morning since Meg and Jake were still too consumed with the little one. Her friends at the theater tried to get her talk several times but eventually gave up, respecting her privacy.

But that didn't stop them from talking, and when Tamara brought up the bachelor auction, Alice froze mid-sweep and stared at the ground.

"That sounds fun," Caitlyn was saying. "Who all is being auctioned off?"

Nicholas. She'd bet her life that the brunette from the gala the other night would scoop him up right away—probably pledge millions just to get her claws into him. She found herself gripping the handle of the broom so hard it hurt.

As much as she'd tossed and turned, she never had come to a conclusion about what she would do. Part of her felt like she was still digesting Meg's words, still sifting through her feelings and the revelations about her mother. She needed to make a decision. Needed to act, but she was frozen. Instead she stood there, uncharacteristically undecided.

What do you know? There was only one thing she knew for certain—she did not want to see Nicholas auctioned off. She couldn't. She might not know how she was going to resolve things with him, but she refused to hand him over to another woman without a fight.

Because I love him. The thought was so jarring she stopped mid-sweep and stared at the room around her in horror.

"Alice, you all right?" Marc asked. Caitlyn and Tamara had stopped what they were doing to turn and stare at her as well.

Alice let out a small choked laugh. After all those hours of thinking and stewing and trying to make sense out of her jumbled emotions, the truth had hit her like a ton of bricks. While she was sweeping a movie theater lobby. All it had taken was the idea of losing him to make her see the truth that had been staring her in the face.

She loved him. Terror and excitement and joy made her breathing shallow and her heart race.

"I think she's going to faint," Tamara whispered.

"Or puke," Caitlyn said. "Where's the mopping bucket?"

Alice waved them away as they came toward her. "I'm not going to throw up. Or faint. I just…I just…" She looked at her friends with wide eyes. Now was the time when she would normally shut down, close herself off. Not because she didn't care about these people—these friends who so obviously cared about her, but because it was part of her stupid protection policy. The fewer people you let in, the less chance of getting hurt. But that was fear talking, and she wouldn't go through life being a coward—not anymore. So she wetted her lips and forced herself to say the words out loud. "I'm in love."

After a heartbeat all three were beaming at her. "Thank God you finally realized it," Caitlyn said.

Alice looked to her in surprise. "You knew?"

Caitlyn rolled her eyes. "Oh please. It was so obvious. I thought you were going to tear my eyes out when you found out we'd gone out on one terrible date."

"Yeah and the way you two were looking at each other in the hospital?" Marc added. "It was like he was your own personal knight in shining armor. The two of you were so sappy in love it would have been gross if it wasn't so cute."

She looked to Tamara, who nodded her agreement. "Kind of gross," she added.

"Gee thanks." But she was laughing despite herself. A heavy weight had lifted from her chest, and her mind seemed to clear. The revelation had cut through the confusion and the mixed emotions. There was still some terror mixed in there, but more than anything she felt clearheaded and...excited.

She could do this. She wasn't weak like her mother. She was strong—like Meg. Now she just had to figure out what she was going to do next, which was easier said than done. But it was a time for new habits and breaking out of her old way of thinking. So she did something she'd never done before. She turned to her friends for help. "You guys, what do I do?"

Cleaning was put on the back burner and a little while later Alice found herself sitting Indian style on the carpeted lobby floor, surrounded by her friends who were listening attentively as she told them everything.

Caitlyn was tearing up by the end, Marc was wide-eyed as if he'd been listening to a fairy tale, and Tamara... Well, Tamara's eyes were unfocused, her chin resting in her hand, as if she was deep in thought. She focused on Tamara, knowing that her dating-averse, quiet friend was thinking this all through and that she would be the voice of reason.

"You've got to tell him how you feel," she said. This was not a shocking revelation. It was common sense. But coming from Tamara's quiet, sincere voice, it felt momentous.

The terror was back in a heartbeat. Especially when she remembered how it had ended the night before—with her walking away from him. He'd told her he loved her and she'd bolted, just like her mother's boyfriends, just the way she feared someone would do to her. She was no better than them.

No, that was her old fears talking. "I walked away from him," she admitted. "I hurt him. What if he doesn't trust me?"

"Then you need to show him how you feel," Caitlyn said.

Marc chimed in with a nod. "You know what they say, actions speak louder than words."

"He needs to know that you're willing to give it a shot, that you're letting him in," Tamara said.

Let me in, Alice, and I'm yours. Her heart squeezed painfully at the memory. Could it really be that easy? "You're right. I have to show him. But how?"

Caitlyn gasped. "The bachelor auction. You could bid on him. Win him back...literally."

Marc clapped his hands together. "That would be so romantic."

The bachelor auction. Her stupid, ridiculous plan that was now mocking her with the fact that she had been willing to give him away to the highest bidder. How had she ever thought that she could let him go?

Tamara's nose scrunched up. "The only problem is that's weeks away. Do you really want to wait that long?"

Alice shook her head. Hell no. But talk of the bachelor auction had her mind racing. The auction was her chance at getting the promotion of her dreams. He'd been willing to walk away from his promotion—for her. That was a sign of trust and commitment. Could she do the same?

It was a no-brainer, really. Of course she could. And she would.

"I'm pulling him from the roster." Her declaration had the other three staring at her.

"But he's the star of the auction, the main event," Caitlyn reminded her.

She nodded quickly. The bachelor auction would never be a success without the golden boy doctor. He was the big draw; the reason the event was already being buzzed about. Pulling him from the lineup would ruin all that and ruin her chance at the promotion. *And she didn't care.* Not if it meant earning his trust—showing him that she was putting her trust in him.

Hell, this was her experience with love and she wasn't going to half-ass it. She'd never backed away from a risk before. Why would she start now? Go big or go home, right? Her friends interrupted her internal pep talk.

"His promotion is riding on this event too, isn't it?" Marc asked.

"And the children's clinic," Tamara reminded her.

Well, shit. She could sacrifice her own promotion, but could she really endanger the clinic's success? How could she live with herself?

And then there was his promotion—yes, he'd offered to walk away from it for her, but that should be his decision. She couldn't just take it from him. Just because he'd offered to walk away from it didn't mean she wanted to steal his chance. It should be his decision. Their decision.

She let out a string of curses under her breath, her lips puckered in a scowl as she toyed with one of the cleaning rags that was sitting on the ground beside her. Her friends were sitting in silence, and they all looked lost in thought, trying to find a solution.

How could she get him out of the auction and not ruin the entire event? The only option would be to find someone to take his place—someone with equal draw. A flicker of hope had her sitting up straight, and her friends' eyes were on her.

"What if I could get someone better?" she asked.

All their eyes widened with excitement...and a question. "Who?" Marc asked.

She racked her brain, trying to think of all of her connections. It wasn't until her gaze fell on Tamara that the answer clicked into place. "Gregory Blanchard."

Tamara's eyes grew comically wide, and color rose in her cheeks. "Gregory?" The name came out as a screech.

The movie theater's new owner was perfect. Excitement had Alice rising to her feet, no longer able to keep still. Tamara and the others rose as well, and Caitlyn and Marc seemed to share her excitement. It was only Tamara who continued to stare in wide-eyed horror.

He was her boss, and from what she'd heard from her friend to date, he was a bossy one at that. But it wasn't like she was asking Tamara to date him, though she did need her friend's help.

"Do you think you could talk to him?" she asked. "Convince him to participate?"

Tamara chewed on her lower lip. "Gregory Blanchard?" she said again, her tone hesitant and strained.

Alice grabbed her friend's hands. "Think about it, Tam, he's perfect. Rich, hot, and available? Not to mention, he's going to be in the top five of Manhattan's most eligible bachelors list, if not in the number one position. He always is."

"He is?" Tamara's brow furrowed in confusion, and Alice rolled her eyes. Her friend was woefully out of touch with the gossip pages.

"Of course he is. He's a billionaire, and he's a bachelor. If we could get him to do this, it would be the event of the season. Of the year!"

Tamara still looked wary but she was nibbling on her lip, clearly deep in thought.

"And just think what good exposure it would be for the theater," Caitlyn added.

Tamara hesitated briefly before nodding. "He does want to get more exposure for the theater with fundraisers and private events."

"So maybe he'd say yes…if you sold it as a business proposition."

Her heart leaped for joy as she saw her friend's posture shift and a resolute look fill her eyes. "Okay, I'll do it. I'll talk to him. But I can't promise anything."

"He'll do it," Alice said as she pulled her friend in for a hug. "Who could deny you anything?"

"Certainly not Gregory," Marc said, his tone teasing.

She caught a funny look between him and Tamara, but then it passed and she had to get out of there. She had to find Nicholas and tell him she'd been wrong—so very wrong.

Nerves and excitement had her racing out of the theater and catching a cab uptown—it wasn't every day one had to face their fears and leap off a cliff. But that was exactly what she was about to do.

She just hoped Nicholas would be there to catch her when she fell.

* * * *

Nicholas stared at the empty pizza box on the floor in front of him. He'd been up all night and at some point had called a twenty-four-hour pizza place for a delivery in the middle of the night and had just polished it off for breakfast, unable to contemplate leaving his apartment long enough to grab breakfast. Was this what depression was? It sure as hell felt like it.

For the millionth time he picked up his phone and started to type in Alice's name to call her. He stopped himself just in time. It was in her hands now, isn't that what Claudia had said?

He had to wait for her to come around. Wait and see if she could bring herself to trust him, to open herself up to him. He had to wait.

Bullshit. He couldn't wait any longer. He'd never been the type to sit around and wait—he was the guy who made things happen. He shoved himself up off the floor and grabbed for his winter jacket, ignoring the fact that he was wearing ratty old sweats.

He would find her, and he would talk to her, and he would... What? Make her love him? He paused mid-step on the way to the door. What did he think he could do? Maybe Claudia was right and it was out of his hands, but there was no way he could just sit here passively and wait. He had to see her, talk to her... He had to do something.

And with that he crossed the rest of the distance to the door and threw it open. He inhaled quickly at the vision before him.

Hand raised to knock, Alice was frozen in his doorway, her eyes wide with surprise at his sudden appearance. "H-hi," she said.

His hands itched to reach out and pull her into his arms. He wanted nothing more than to kiss her senseless, he was so freakin' happy to see her. But then he registered her appearance, and concern rapidly overshadowed his excitement.

Dark circles shadowed her red-rimmed eyes. She hadn't slept either, and she'd clearly been crying. Her hair was pulled off her face in a ponytail that made her look younger, more vulnerable than he'd ever seen her before. And her clothes... She was wearing an oversized T-shirt and ill-fitting jeans—as if she'd borrowed someone else's clothes. Jesus, had she even made it home the night before?

He opened the door wider. "Come on in."

She led the way inside and paused as if hesitant to go any farther. It was her first time in his apartment, he realized with a start. Funny how much had happened between them in such a short period of time.

Crazy hope had adrenaline coursing through him, making him unable to stop moving despite the fact that he hadn't slept all night. Maybe Claudia had been right—she would come around given a little time. She'd changed her mind. He hurried around the room cleaning some of the junk off the surfaces and throwing it into a pile in his bedroom. He cleared the pizza box off the couch and gestured for her to sit down while he went to throw it away.

When he came back into the living room, Alice was standing exactly where he'd left her, still as a statue. Some of the hope dampened. She didn't look like a woman who was about to declare her love. She sure as hell didn't look like she'd changed her mind. Her expression was grim, her mouth set in a firm line.

She looked determined and stressed out—not exactly a harbinger of romantic declarations.

He tried to steel himself for what was to come, crossing his arms over his chest and forcing a hardness into his tone. "What are you doing here, Alice?"

Her eyes turned up to his, and for a second he thought he saw a flicker of panic, but then she opened her mouth to speak, and he forgot all about her fear. "I'm here to talk about the fundraiser."

Any remaining hope flickered and died and the void it left behind was filled with sudden irrational anger. The fundraiser? The bloody effing fundraiser. He should have known that was what she was worried about. That was the only reason she was here. A cold, harsh laugh escaped him, and he ran his hand over his face. Here he'd spent the night rehashing every word they'd ever exchanged, agonizing over what he could have done differently, how he could have gotten through to her.

And she'd spent the night worrying about her job security.

"I don't think that you—" she started.

He cut her off, unable to hear whatever it was she had to say. "Don't worry about it."

She blinked at him, her brows temporarily lowering in confusion.

God, he couldn't stand to see her there in his apartment looking so lovely and so sweet when he could never have her. He needed her gone.

"Don't worry," he said again. "What happened last night won't affect the fundraiser. I'll still go through with my part of the bargain."

She opened her mouth and closed it. He watched her lick her lips as if nervous.

Of course she was nervous, her precious career was on the line. Misery made his tone more biting than he intended. "It might be fun, actually."

Her eyes widened with surprise, and he forced himself to ignore the draw they had on him. He'd been a sucker, a fool. Well, no more. "Who knows. Maybe I'll meet my future wife at the auction. There are a lot of eligible young women who actually want to be with me."

Oh God, he sounded pathetic, trying to make her jealous. Trying to prove that he had something to give.

"I know, I—" Her soft voice cut straight through him. It was sadness he heard, or maybe pity.

He hurried on, unable to stand the idea that she felt sorry for him—the man she rejected. "You were right last night, you know."

"I was?" She stared up at him with wide, unblinking eyes.

He nodded, hating himself for wanting to punish her. "Mmm. You were right that I deserve someone who isn't afraid of commitment. Someone who wants the same things that I want in life."

He watched for her response. *Argue with me! Tell me I'm wrong.* But she just nodded jerkily. "You do," she whispered.

He nodded. That was it then. She'd confirmed it. Nothing had changed; she was still trying to push him toward other women. Women he didn't want or need. Not like he needed her.

He forced himself to draw in a deep breath despite the stabbing pain in his chest. "I think you should leave."

She nodded again, backing up toward the door before turning and racing toward it as if she was running for her life.

When the door closed behind her, Nicholas let out the breath he'd been holding, but the pain didn't ease. It grew so intense he thought his heart might be splitting in two.

Chapter 12

Alice hated herself. Self-hate combined with self-pity led to two empty pints of ice cream sitting atop Ena's coffee table as she remained curled up in a ball on one side of the couch, Ena patting her leg on the other.

"Now, now," Ena said. "You're making too big a deal of this."

"Too big a deal?" Alice turned her eyes from *An American in Paris*, which was failing miserably at its job of cheering her up, to look at Ena. "I ruined it. I ruined everything. I meant to go there and tell Nicholas I loved him and… I couldn't do it."

Ena looked toward her door. "Then why not go over there right now? He's probably sitting over there in his apartment feeling just as miserable."

"He's not," Alice said with a pathetic sigh. "He's at the hospital."

Ena gave her a questioning look and Alice felt herself flush beneath the stare. "I asked Carl to keep tabs on him," she mumbled.

While Carl may have his moral standards on handing out information on Alice, he seemed to have no qualms about spying on the nice doctor. Ena's mouth was pinched, but some snorts of laughter escaped through her nose.

Alice made a show of ignoring her amusement. This was not a laughing matter! She'd finally fallen in love, and she'd finally admitted it to herself—and then she'd let it slip between her fingers.

Ena gave her another pat of consolation. "You'll have another chance to talk to him and make this right."

Alice turned to her friend and didn't even try to hide the desperate sadness. "But what if he was right? He said he deserved better…."

"Nonsense. He was angry and hurt, but he told you he loves you. A man doesn't change his mind that quickly, especially not a kind, loyal, trustworthy man like Nicholas."

Maybe she was right. Hope flickered in her belly… But hope was a dangerous thing. She didn't think she could handle another disappointment.

Still, she found herself practically begging for reassurance. "You really think so?"

Ena gave a little snort of amusement. "Of course. You're right on track, as far as I'm concerned."

Alice frowned at her. "Right on track?"

Her elderly friend gestured toward the TV screen. "This is how it always happens, you know. There's always one last big misunderstanding just before the hero and heroine finally get together. It builds anticipation and makes the final scene—the one where they finally kiss—that much more satisfying."

Alice found herself torn between amusement and disbelief. Amusement won out and for the first time in the twenty-four hours since that disastrous encounter, she found herself laughing. "You don't really believe that, do you? You can't possibly think that real life resembles old musicals in any way."

Ena was laughing too, but she wagged a finger in Alice's direction. "Don't discount happy endings, my dear. They happen all the time. Oh, they're usually a bit messier, and they're not the final ending, life goes on after the big kiss—but happy endings aren't complete fiction."

Alice rolled her eyes but she couldn't deny that she was feeling a bit more heartened. Maybe it was just the laughter or maybe it was the dance sequence that was currently playing, but a bit of optimism seemed to have crept its way into her heart, easing some of the pain.

Maybe all hope wasn't lost. Maybe she still stood a chance.

They still had to work on the fundraiser together, which meant he wasn't completely out of her life. Not yet, at least. She still had a shot—and she would take it.

* * * *

She made her move the very next day. Monday morning she asked her assistant to set an urgent meeting with Dixon, Jamison, and Nicholas. He couldn't refuse if the meeting was work related and came from her bosses. He'd made it clear that he was still determined to make a success of this fundraiser and she would use that to her advantage.

Her heart was racing as her boss and his boss entered the conference room, cheerful and chatting, and apparently unaware that she was a trembling wreck of nerves. She must have been a better actress than she knew because neither of them seemed suspicious of her behavior as they all sat and waited for Nicholas.

What if he didn't come? Surely he had to. She'd made sure his schedule was clear, she knew he had no patients that morning. He would come, if for no other reason than to make sure the clinic's fundraiser was a success.

And he did show, albeit five nerve-wracking minutes late. He strode into the conference room looking dashing as ever, confident as usual... but disheveled. Well, disheveled for Nicholas, which wasn't really all that disheveled. He sported a light five-o'clock shadow and his eyes looked shadowed, tired. Like he too hadn't slept all weekend.

Alice clasped her hands in front of her on the conference room table and ordered herself to slow down. *Do not let yourself get too hopeful. This could still fail.* But she wouldn't let this go without at least trying. Because Meg was right, she wasn't like their mother. She was brave, dammit, and she would fight for what she wanted. And what she wanted was Nicholas.

"Thank you for coming, gentlemen," she started, her voice shockingly calm and cool considering her rapid heart rate. "This won't take long. I just wanted to keep you all up to date on the progress of the children's clinic fundraiser."

Her bosses were watching her with mild curiosity but Nicholas, she noted, was staring at her with narrowed eyes, as if he were suspicious... or angry. Neither of which would be unwarranted, really. She hadn't expected him to come in here with a smile, but still the lack of his typical kindness and warmth left her cold. She shivered slightly beneath his stare before flipping open the notebook she'd set on the table. It was filled with random notes and to-do lists, but she focused on it as if it held the secrets of the universe. If she wasn't looking directly at him, perhaps she could get through this without losing her nerve.

She started with the basics, reading a list of the donors who'd confirmed their attendance, giving them an update on the logistics that she, the catering company, and Tamara had worked out. Once that was done, there was no more procrastinating. She risked one quick glance up and met Nicholas's shuttered, unreadable expression.

"And one more thing," she said. "There's been a change to the agenda for the bachelor auction."

There was a silence in the room, and Alice couldn't bring herself to look up again, though she could feel Nicholas's eyes on her.

She swallowed thickly. "Nicholas is no longer our star bachelor. Gregory Blanchard has agreed to participate."

Dixon's and Jamison's reactions were instantaneous and delighted. "What a coup!" "How did you ever convince him?" "Great work, Alice." But all the praise and questions went straight past her. She'd lifted her eyes and met Nicholas's stare. She could practically see his brain working, making connections. She saw confusion and...and hope.

Her heart squeezed painfully in her chest. Maybe she wasn't too late after all. *Please, God, say I'm not too late.*

She licked her dry lips and kept eye contact. "Nicholas, I know you never loved the idea of being part of this auction. So this means you no longer have to participate…if you don't want to."

Understanding dawned in his eyes then, and the blaze of emotions she saw there left her breathless.

"Gentlemen, would you mind giving us a minute?" Nicholas asked, his eyes never leaving hers. "Alice and I still have some details to hash out."

Dixon and Jamison agreed, getting up hastily and parting with words of congratulations on landing the bachelor of the year.

When the door shut behind them, the silence was deafening.

Nicholas stood and came around to her side of the table. She stood too, but her knees were so wobbly she had to keep one hand on the back of her chair for support. She could do this, she could. She was strong like Meg.

Nicholas stopped in front of her, so close she could smell his familiar scent and feel his warmth. She wanted to collapse into his arms, have him tell her he loved her, and then she could say it, too.

But he deserved better. She had to be the one to say it this time. She had to show him that she could be brave…that she could trust. That she *did* trust him.

"What does this mean, Alice?" he said, his voice so low and gruff she nearly didn't hear him.

She swallowed the last of her fear. "I don't want to lose you." It wasn't the speech she'd intended to make but the truth came out of its own volition. Tears sprang to her eyes as she continued. "You were right the other night. You deserve someone better than me. Someone who doesn't have trust issues…." She paused to catch her breath, the emotions in his eyes making it difficult to breathe. "But I'm selfish. I want a chance." She reached out for him then, gripping his sweater in her hands. "I'm not giving you up without a fight, and I'm certainly not going to just hand you over to some—"

His lips crushed hers, cutting off her speech as he kissed her as if their lives depended on it. She met his kiss eagerly, her lips clinging to his, parting for his tongue, which claimed her mouth with a possessiveness that made her knees go weak.

He held her to him, holding her up. She tore her lips away only briefly. She wasn't done. She had to say it. "I love you, Nicholas."

He groaned, kissing her once more, but this time murmuring words of love between kisses. His words and touch erasing the last of her fear. When he pulled back briefly to look at her, that beautiful kindness and warmth once again back in his gaze and focused on her, she tried to speak again. "I'm sorry, Nicholas. I'm so sorry." He shushed her, one arm holding her close by the waist while he used his free hand to tangle in her hair and tilt her head up so her eyes met his.

"Don't apologize," he said. "Do you trust me?"

She didn't hesitate. "I do."

He grinned then, and the force of it made her insides melt into a puddle. "Then we'll be all right," he said. "We'll figure it out as we go, and we'll figure it out together."

Alice nodded, believing him and believing in herself for the first time in forever. "I may not be very good at this relationship stuff." She felt compelled to warn him.

His laugh was low and husky and warmed her to her core. "I think you'll be better at it than you expect."

His words warmed her, giving her more confidence. "And why is that?"

He dipped his head to nuzzle the sensitive skin beneath her ear, making her gasp for air. "Because you've already conquered the biggest hurdle," he said. He paused to trail kisses along her neck. "You're trusting me with your heart, just like I'm trusting you with mine."

She couldn't tell if it was his words, the kisses, or the sheer relief that her plan had worked that had her breathless and light-headed. "So what do we do now?"

He pulled back so he could meet her gaze, his eyes dark with desire. "I suggest you concoct another 'family emergency' so we can head back to my place. There is no way I can let you out of my arms today. Or tomorrow. We may both need to take a leave of absence from work from the foreseeable future."

She was laughing as his lips claimed hers once more. When they parted for air, she said, "I am all for playing hooky, Nicholas, but I meant in general. Like, what do we do now?"

Some of the terror was still there, making the butterflies in her stomach flutter at the scary unknown that lay before them. But this fear was no longer debilitating, and it sure as hell wouldn't hold her back. And for all the fear, there was an equal amount of excitement that had her pulse racing, eager to see what lay in store for them next.

Nicholas's eyes met hers, and she watched his lips twitching with amusement. "What do we do now?" he echoed before shaking his head. "You know, Alice, for the first time in my life, I have no idea what comes next."

She grinned up at him and looped her arms around his neck. "Kinda scary, right?"

He nodded. "Oh, it's terrifying."

Laughter bubbled up inside of her, breaking down the last remnants of those walls she'd always held so dear. The ones that had once kept the world at bay. She tugged his head down to place a quick, hard kiss on his lips. "Well, whatever happens next, at least we're in it together."

That earned her another long, thorough kiss that had her flushed and feverish. Which really worked in her favor when she went to tell her bosses that she was so sick she just had to work from home—for the rest of the week.

Epilogue

The bachelor auction was a smashing success by anyone's standards. For Alice, the highlight was being able to watch all the fun with her new boyfriend at her side. As the last of the bachelors were snapped up by the crowd of zealous women, Nicholas leaned down to whisper in her ear, "Now, aren't you glad you didn't sell me off to the highest bidder?"

The feel of his warm breath on her bare neck sent shivers through her and she linked her hand through his, eager for physical contact, even if it could only be hand holding since they were in public.

Nicholas seemed to read her mind. "When does the dancing start up?"

She grinned up at him. "Soon. Why? Are you so eager to show off our new moves?" He'd surprised her the week before with an early birthday present—ballroom dance lessons for the two of them. They'd only had one lesson so far, but the sheer thoughtfulness of the gift still made her heart leap for joy whenever she thought about it.

He was laughing as he pulled her into his arms, apparently not caring that they were in public. "I'm excited to show you off," he said. "My new girlfriend."

She couldn't stop the giddy smile at the simple words.

He leaned in close and whispered, "My new girlfriend, and my last."

Tears pricked the back of her eyes. But then, why should she be surprised? It seemed that after nearly two decades of not shedding any tears, her tear ducts were trying to make up for it. She seemed to forever be losing her composure around this guy—her boyfriend—though luckily the tears were usually ones of happiness, like right now. "The last girlfriend, huh?" she teased. "That sounds ominous."

He let out a long, melodramatic sigh. "It's true, I'm afraid. My bachelor days are rapidly coming to an end. You're it…. You're the one."

She was too choked up to speak, and he drew back to look at her expression. "Uh oh. I promised myself I wouldn't move too quickly and scare you off. I didn't, did I?"

She shook her head quickly. No, she wasn't scared. His words struck her heart and resonated. "Not scared," she said. "Just happy."

As if on cue, the band struck up a song and dancers started to make their way onto the makeshift dance floor in the lobby. Alice took Nicholas by the hand and tugged him toward the other dancers. "Come on, Hot Doc. Let's show them what we've got."

He was laughing as he fell into his place in front of her, pulling her into his arms so they could move together in time to the music. She let her eyes shut briefly as she lost herself in the melody, and the movement, and the feel of his strong arms around her.

"What are you thinking?" he asked, his voice soft and gentle and kind—just like Nicholas.

She opened her eyes and smiled up at him. "I was just thinking about something that Ena said once."

He raised one brow in question.

"She said that happy endings weren't just for the movies. And right now? Well, now I know that she was right."

His arms tightened around her, and he leaned down until his lips crushed hers. She met the urgency of his kiss and held on tight, heedless of the other dancers or the fact that they were no longer in time with the music. But it didn't matter because they were holding on to each other and neither of them would ever let go.

Don't miss Maggie Dallen's A Chance Romance series.

The Accidental Engagement

Oops . . .

It started as a regular night for New York City restaurant hostess Ivy Sinclair, until a rowdy customer turned out to be world famous playboy Jack Everett. Thanks to the paparazzi, now the world thinks they're a couple—which couldn't be farther from the truth. But when a brooding, sexy businessman offers her a simply irresistible proposition...

Uh oh . . .

Just when cutthroat venture capitalist Daniel Gladwell thought he'd never close the deal with an Italian conglomerate, a simple mistake becomes the perfect opportunity. All he has to do is convince Ivy to pretend to be Jack's fiancée while on a business trip to Italy to offset Jack's bad boy reputation. As long as Daniel doesn't sabotage the plan by claiming the tempting waitress for himself . . .

Oh yes!

It was supposed to be a business only arrangement. But in the magic of the Tuscan countryside, neither Ivy nor Daniel can fight the attraction building between them. In the world's most romantic setting, the line between business and pleasure is one that begs to be crossed . . .

Chapter 1

Ivy Sinclair thought she'd seen it all as a hostess at a hotel bar—but when a young man came running up to her with a look of panic before diving behind her hostess stand—well, now she'd really seen everything.

"Excuse me, can I help you?" she asked, looking down at the top of his head as he crouched beside her.

The young man barely looked at her. He was too busy peering around the edge of the stand toward the door. He muttered a curse as a large, brutish man wearing an intimidating scowl walked in.

"I'm not here," the young man at her feet whispered.

"Excuse me?"

"Please," he added. His eyes widened and filled with panic. Ivy couldn't help but take pity.

The large man who looked ready to kill zeroed in on her. "Where is he?"

She swallowed a lump of fear at the aggressive tone. "Where is who?" Ivy tried to keep her voice innocent but it came out as a squeak.

She cleared her throat and tried again. "I'm afraid I don't know to whom you're referring."

He leaned in closer and Ivy fought the impulse to run. "Where is Everett?" he growled.

Ivy stared down the oversized thug who was leaning over the hostess stand. She tried not to flinch even as his hot, rancid breath hit her square in the face.

"As I said before, sir, I have no idea what you're talking about."

Several guests had paused in the hotel lobby, en route to the restaurant to watch the drama unfold. The giant didn't seem to mind the attention but this job was Ivy's only source of income and she could repeat the manager's lecture on courtesy and service verbatim. But above all else, her job was to be discreet.

Ivy had to believe that meant covering for the well-dressed, albeit rumpled young man who was currently crouching behind the hostess stand, uncomfortably close to her legs. She didn't know what the hidden man had done but she couldn't blame him for hiding from the heavyset giant who loomed over her—he looked like a man who was capable of causing serious pain.

And at this particular moment he looked like he would throttle her given the slightest provocation. Ivy was a good foot shorter than the brute, with a petite frame—not exactly an even match. She tried to keep her voice soft but stern—the same tone she used to cajole Otis, her parents' German Shepherd, into his cage when it was time to visit the vet.

"I don't know what this Mr.—uh—"

"Everett. Jack Everett," the man sneered.

The name caused even more passersby to stop in their tracks. *Why did that name sound familiar?*

"I don't know what Mr. Everett has done, but I assure you I have not seen the man you described come into this restaurant."

His frown deepened into a menacing glare and she added, "If Mr. Everett comes looking for you, I'd be happy to pass along a message, Mr.—"

He leaned in even closer. "You tell Jack that if I see him with my wife again, he's a dead man."

Ivy's hands clenched at her side. That was it. She couldn't have people making death threats in her restaurant. She drew a deep breath and mustered her courage. "If you don't leave immediately, I'm afraid I'll be forced to call the police."

The burly man slammed a fist against the podium. "Listen, lady, I'll do whatever I—" His voice cut off abruptly when she snatched up the phone and started dialing, keeping eye contact all the while.

The man muttered a curse, shook his head, and backed toward the door. "You tell that little bastard I'm coming for him."

When she was certain the man was gone from view, Ivy let out a deep breath and looked down at the young man.

"You are my hero," he said with a grin.

Ivy rolled her eyes and reached out a hand to help him to his feet. "You're Jack, I presume?"

The young man paused on his knees, a lock of floppy brown hair partially covering eyes that were filled with mischief.

"If I were you, I would get out of here quick, before he comes back," she said.

He ignored her advice and grasped her hands in his. "I'm serious, I owe you my life. That guy was going to kill me."

Ivy stifled a laugh at his melodramatic tone. He looked to be around the same age as her—most likely in his late twenties—but everything from his laughing eyes to his mussed hair said he was a little boy in a grown man's body.

"In case you didn't hear, that nice gentleman would prefer that you stay away from his wife. I hope you take his advice," she added, allowing honesty to outweigh discretion for a moment.

His look was sheepish and he gave her an adorable lopsided grin but he made no attempt to deny the accusations. The man had the face of a movie star and clearly the charm and confidence to go with it. She shouldn't be surprised that he was a ladies' man. Working in a hotel restaurant she'd witnessed more than her fair share of adulterous rendezvous. She'd thought she was worldly-wise when she'd first started working at the hotel. She was no longer fresh off the bus from her tiny hometown in Ohio, but she'd still been shocked by the constant and casual affairs. Now, after two years in one of New York's swankiest hotels her scandalized disgust had given way to weary disapproval.

The young man was still on his knees and resisted her insistent tug. She was horrified to realize that the crowd of people who'd gathered to witness the earlier scene were now watching *her*—with more than a little amusement. Heat flooded her cheeks and she dipped her head. "Please stand up," she muttered.

He flashed her a wicked grin. "Not until you accept my sincere gratitude—"

"Fine, you're welcome. Now stand up, please."

"And tell me how I can repay you," he finished.

"You can repay me by standing up." Whether it was her pleading tone or the red cheeks, he did stand up—and planted a sloppy kiss on her lips.

Sputtering with surprise and embarrassment, she pushed him away and turned her face from the people who were now laughing and clapping. Ivy ducked her head, trying to hide her flaming cheeks behind a curtain of hair. She grabbed Jack by the hand and dragged him into the hallway leading to the restrooms, away from the prying eyes of strangers. "What do you think you're doing?"

"Sorry," he drawled. "I just wanted to say thank you." His eyes were wide with innocence but the unapologetic grin told her that he found her distress entertaining.

"You've said it," Ivy said with a scowl. She tugged her hand out of his and crossed her arms into her chest.

His lips twitched in what she assumed was a valiant attempt to keep from laughing. "Do you know who I am?"

Ivy blinked at the sudden turn in conversation. "According to your friend who was just here, I'd assume you're Jack Everett."

He crossed his arms and leaned back, his eyes searching her face, waiting for something—some sort of recognition, no doubt. The hotel where she worked was one of the most exclusive in the city; nearly every guest thought they were famous as well as rich. They were almost always wrong.

"Should that mean something to me?" she asked.

"Nothing," he said with a laugh. "Nothing at all. So now that we've established my name, why don't you tell me yours?"

"Ivy Sinclair."

"As in poison ivy?"

"As in The Holly and the Ivy." At his raised eyebrow, she explained. "My mom has a thing for Christmas."

"Don't tell me you have a sister named Holly," he teased. She gave a sheepish shrug and he burst out laughing.

He gave a jaunty salute as he walked back toward the hotel lobby. "Thank you for saving my life, Ivy Sinclair. I'll be in touch."

* * * *

Word had spread quickly in the hotel and less than twenty minutes after Jack left, Ivy had been summoned to the manager's office. Franklin Webster was known for being a tough boss but he kept his mouth shut through the entire tale, giving her a chance to fully explain her side of the story.

Ivy cleared her throat and forced herself to continue despite Franklin's intimidating frown. "So you see, sir, I really didn't intend to cause such a scene. I was trying my best to keep the situation under wraps. But this young man…well, I'm afraid he was a bit of a ham and he sort of made me—er, *us*—the center of attention."

When she'd finished explaining, he took his time polishing his glasses and made a show of straightening his tie. Ivy tried not to squirm in her seat. Every time she was called into Franklin's office she couldn't help but feel like she'd been called in to see the principal. More nerve-wracking since the only times she was called on to speak to the principal were when her sister Holly was in trouble.

"Ivy, do you have any idea who Jack Everett is?"

Ivy's eyes widened in surprise. "Uh, no sir."

Franklin sighed. He handed her a copy of one of the tabloids that were sold in the hotel's gift shop.

Ivy stared at the front cover, momentarily speechless. There he was—the man who'd huddled by her feet while she fended off an angry husband. He was flashing the camera that now-familiar cocky grin, one hand on the back of a supermodel as they made their way toward a waiting limo. "Tech Mogul Out on the Town," the headline read. Ivy had never taken much interest in gossip columns or celebrities and today her willful ignorance was on display.

When she looked up she saw that Franklin was watching her with a tight-lipped look of disapproval. "I'd say your Mr. Everett has a tendency to find the spotlight. Or rather, the spotlight has a tendency to find him."

Ivy let out a pent up breath. "So you're not angry?"

"No, I'm not angry. I think you handled the whole thing quite well, considering...."

"Oh, thank you, Mr. Webster," Ivy interrupted.

Franklin's lips twisted into a rare hint of a smile. "Of course. And if Mr. Everett should be true to his offer and come back to the hotel, I know you will do everything in your power to keep him...*entertained.*"

The suggestion made Ivy's skin crawl but her smile didn't falter. It remained frozen in place as her stomach churned. She had heard stories about coworkers being urged to dress more provocatively or to flirt with the guests but she never believed them to be true. She struggled to keep her voice even. "Excuse me?"

His expression remained coy. "I think you know what I mean, my dear." His gaze lowered and he studied her figure as though appraising a piece of art at auction. "My sources tell me you were quite a hit with the young man."

She forced a joking tone as she held the tabloid up before her. "From what I gather, most women are a hit with that young man."

Franklin let out a cackle that made her jump in her seat. Franklin Webster did not laugh. Everyone knew that. But at least he wasn't eyeing her like a piece of meat anymore.

He settled back into his seat. "I like you, Ivy. You're smart and you're a go-getter. This is a tough business and there aren't a lot of openings in the areas where you show an interest..." his voice trailed off and he seemed to be weighing how best to phrase the next statement. "You'll soon learn that to be considered for promotion, an employee must show that he or she is willing to go above and beyond for the company."

Bile rose in her throat. She was going to be sick. She knew exactly what he was insinuating but feigned confusion. "Mr. Webster, are you suggesting that I get involved in a romantic relationship with Mr. Everett for the sake of my job?"

Franklin's mouth opened and closed to resemble a guppy as he protested the coarse accusation. "Of course not. I would never suggest such a thing."

"Of course not," she repeated—*because that would be illegal.*

Feeling a twinge of success at having the last word, she made a move to leave the office but he stopped her.

"No one would ever make such a crass suggestion at this hotel," he said. "But I hope you keep in mind, my dear, that there are a limited number of jobs at this hotel and there is no room for employees who aren't team players."

She stopped in her tracks halfway to the door with her back to the manager. The threat could hardly be called "veiled".

Panic warred with disgust. She needed this job.

She heard the crinkle of the tabloid when he picked it up. "We're willing to overlook your antics this afternoon because we know that you are a team player. Am I making myself clear?"

Ivy resisted the urge to spin around and tell the old man where he could shove the tabloid and her job. But that couldn't happen. She could barely afford to pay this month's rent and she was drowning in debt from her stint on unemployment. And there was no way she could turn to her parents. They had enough on their plate trying to keep their house. The last thing they needed was another mouth to feed.

It was only the thought of having to run back to her parents that gave her the strength to turn around and force a smile. "Understood, Mr. Webster."

* * * *

Ivy's studio apartment in Brooklyn was tiny, but it was all hers, and for that she was eternally grateful. Particularly that evening when all she wanted was a hot bath and a glass of wine.

Hours had passed and she still couldn't get rid of the disgusted feeling. Not even a hot bath could wash it away. For what felt like the millionth time that week, Ivy considered quitting. Oh, it would feel so good. She sank further into the tub and let herself daydream about all the ways she could give her notice. In reality, she would go to bed, wake up, and do it all over again.

She'd moved to the city right after college because she'd landed a great job in an up-and-coming ad agency. But less than two years into the great new job, the recession had hit, and Ivy's entire office had been liquidated. Hers was a small branch of a large company and the closure of their office had been a necessary sacrifice for the greater good—or so she'd been told.

The hostess gig wasn't exactly her dream job but it paid the bills and it was steady work after a series of temp jobs. And it wasn't *all* bad. More and more lately she'd been called in to help the assistant manager with event planning for the hotel and she'd discovered it was something she really enjoyed. She knew there was an opening for an events manager at the hotel. If she could just keep her head down and hold her tongue with Franklin, the job could be hers.

She sighed and sipped her wine. That was a very big "if."

The front door buzzer rang just as she was stepping out of the tub. Her elderly neighbor Edith liked to stop in for a cup of tea and a chat often and she always seemed to show up at a time when Ivy craved solitude. Sleepy and wet from the bath, she threw on a robe and went to answer the door. She tried to summon a smile for her elderly friend.

"Hi Ed—" The name stuck in her throat as she faced the stranger in her doorway.

This visitor was *not* a harmless old woman.

Ivy's mouth gaped as she took in the tall man with dark hair and even darker eyes. His shoulders were broad and he wore a well-tailored suit that looked incongruous in the dingy hallway of her apartment building. Behind him stood a nondescript man with an earpiece and ramrod posture.

"Miss Sinclair?" The tall man before her smiled, causing his eyes to crinkle and eased the intimidation factor only slightly.

"Yes?" Ivy cinched her robe tighter. She was keenly aware of the fact that she wore nothing beneath her flimsy robe.

"I'm Daniel Gladwell, I work with Jack Everett. I believe you met him this afternoon?"

Ivy nodded, unable to take her eyes off of the man before her. He had the kind of chiseled features that were usually reserved for statues or actors portraying James Bond. She made a futile attempt to swipe away some of the unruly auburn curls that had escaped from the loose bun atop her head.

She closed the door a little behind her and took a step into the hallway, wary now that the surprise of finding a gorgeous man in her doorway had worn off.

"Can I help you with something?"

The man's smile grew and he tilted his chin in a charming sort of aw-shucks way, but it was all show—the look in his eyes was strictly business. "Actually, I believe you can. May I come in?"

Ivy hesitated; her small town politeness warred with practical street smarts. "I'd rather not invite strange men into my apartment."

"Of course." If he was surprised to be denied, he didn't let on. "I apologize for the late hour. Jack just informed me of this afternoon's *interaction* and I wanted to speak with you immediately."

Now Ivy was truly intrigued. "Is something the matter? Is Jack okay?"

"Oh no, he's fine. Thanks in no small part to you."

Heat flooded her cheeks under his watchful gaze. Despite his warm smile and easy demeanor, his eyes were calculating and observant. They seemed to take in everything, from her bare feet to the damp tendrils clinging to her neck.

"That's actually why I'm here, Miss Sinclair."

"Call me Ivy, please."

"I wanted to thank you in person for your assistance today. I'm sure you're aware of Jack's fame and fortune—he's easy fodder for the tabloids."

Ivy nodded, but she was sure some of the confusion she felt was evident. *Where on earth was he going with this?* She shifted from one foot to the other.

"I came here tonight because I'd like to show you how appreciative we are...."

"We?"

"My business partners and I. There is a lot invested in Jack, and his reputation."

"I see," Ivy said politely.

"We'd like to show you our appreciation for your help today and for your discretion in the future." He was watching her closely for some sort of reaction and it took several moments for Ivy to fully grasp what he was implying.

"You want to pay me to keep my mouth shut?" The words slipped out before she could stop herself.

Only a slight widening of the eyes revealed Daniel's surprise at her outburst but he recovered quickly. "Well, that's one way of putting it, I suppose."

Daniel gave her a lopsided grin, the first genuine smile she'd seen, and Ivy was very nearly charmed off of her feet.

For a moment she just stared at the man before her, unsure of how she should react. She didn't know whether she was offended or amused. Amusement won out and she startled both men in her hallway when she burst out with a great peal of laughter.

She slapped a hand over her mouth and let out a little snort as she tried to contain her giggles. "Oh, I'm so sorry, this is just too much." She waved her hand toward Daniel and the silent man behind him who was watching her with no expression. "I feel like I just stepped into a movie or something. I mean, are you seriously trying to pay me off? If I don't take it am I going to swim with the fishes?" She giggled again at her own joke.

"Ms. Sin—Ivy, I hope I haven't offended you."

"No, no, why would I be offended?" she said, still smothering a laugh. She took a step back into her apartment and started to close her door. "Thank you for the laugh, Daniel, but you don't need to pay me. I won't say a word." She held up three fingers in salute. "Scout's honor."

His forehead creased in concern as he gave her a doubtful look that said he wasn't convinced. He opened his mouth to protest, but she held up a hand to stop him.

"Look, I understand where you're coming from, I really do. But believe me when I say I have absolutely no interest in that sort of fame. And if you don't believe that, then maybe you'll understand this—the hotel has very strict rules about not speaking to the press about their guests. If I break that rule, I'd be out of a job. If you don't trust my girl scout's honor—which is sacred, by the way—then believe me when I say I would never jeopardize my job."

He studied her for a moment longer and was apparently satisfied with whatever he saw there. "I'm sorry I disturbed you, Ivy. Have a good night."

* * * *

Ivy didn't even have a chance to hang up her coat when she arrived at work the next day; she was summoned to the manager's office the moment she walked through the door.

She was stunned to find Daniel there, leaning against the manager's desk when she walked in. Both he and Franklin turned to look at her when she entered. Ivy's stomach sank. This could not be good.

Franklin was the first to react to her arrival. He threw down a copy of that morning's paper and beckoned her over to take a look. She cautiously edged toward the desk and glanced at the paper spread before her—it was open to the gossip section. Both men seemed to be waiting for a reaction so she took a step closer and looked down.

Ivy's stomach dropped and she leaned in closer, unable to believe what she was seeing. It couldn't be. There was a large color photo in the center of the page that showed Jack on his knees before her with a caption that read, "Renowned bachelor Jack Everett may finally have found his bride. Everyone wants to know—who is the lucky lady?" As if that wasn't bad enough, there was another picture just below that perfectly captured Jack's ridiculous kiss. "Brilliant billionaire smitten with his mystery woman," the caption read.

There was a little blurb beside the pictures but Ivy couldn't tear her gaze away from the image of herself looking like a woman in love. Like a woman being proposed to, no less. This couldn't be happening.... A rush of adrenaline flooded through her, leaving her shaky and lightheaded. The words blurred before her eyes. She had a feeling she didn't want to read whatever they'd printed anyways. There was no way there would be one hint of truth to any of it.

"Franklin, may I have a private word with Ivy, please?" Daniel asked.

It wasn't so much a request as an order. Ivy couldn't believe anyone would dare to kick the old manager out of his own office but Daniel seemed to be the type to take control of every room he was in. The older man, who normally put the fear of God into Ivy, looked weak and nervous beside him. Franklin nodded and hurried toward the door. Daniel's face gave nothing away but Franklin's tight-lipped grimace was more than enough to tell her that she was in trouble. When he passed her on the way out of his office he shot out a hand and gripped her arm roughly. "You will do whatever he says to make this right, do you understand me?"

Ivy nodded and swallowed. This was it—she was going to lose her job.

Daniel leaned against the desk, one leg crossed in front of the other. He was wearing another perfectly tailored suit. This one was a dark gray as opposed to the jet-black suit he'd worn the night before in her hallway but it fit just as well. He was perfectly groomed from the tidy hair to the shined designer shoes. Unlike most men she knew, he looked like he was comfortable in formal attire as though he had been born and raised wearing designer business suits.

He was watching her. His dark eyes scrutinized her every move, and despite his relaxed posture, or maybe because of it, Ivy grew unbearably tense until she had to do something.

The words came spilling out of her mouth. "I had nothing to do with that," she said, pointing to the newspaper. Her shaking hand seemed to betray her, making her look guilty rather than what she was—horrified. She instantly regretted the outburst. She hated how defensive she sounded.

Daniel nodded, his expression unreadable. "I know."

Ivy shifted uncomfortably. Well, at least he knew she wasn't the enemy here. "If you'd like for me to call the newspaper, explain what happened…."

Daniel shook his head. "Unfortunately, the situation is a little too complicated for that."

Ivy's face scrunched up in confusion. "Too complicated for the truth?"

She thought she saw a flicker of amusement in his eyes but it was fleeting. He gestured to the chair in front of him. "Please, have a seat and I'll explain."

Ivy hesitated for a moment before squaring her shoulders, and perching on the edge of the chair. She tried to discreetly pull down the hem of her skirt, which suddenly felt much too short under his scrutinizing gaze.

He sat across from her and leaned over the desk with his hands folded. Every gesture, every move, was precise. This was a man who thought through everything—nothing was unintentional or improvised. Everything was planned. And the way he was looking at her now? It was clear he had a plan for her.

"As I mentioned last night, my company has a lot at stake, and it's all riding on Jack. He is the face of EverTech and his reputation has a direct impact on the business."

Ivy nodded and tried not to shift in her seat. *Just get to the point already.*

"I won't beat around the bush, Ivy."

Oh God, could he read minds?

"I am in the middle of negotiating a very sensitive merger with a company that could either make or break EverTech."

When he paused Ivy wondered if she was supposed to speak. She opened her mouth, about to ask what any of this had to do with her but he continued before she could get the words out.

"The owner of the other company, Gianni Brunelli—well, he's a bit old-fashioned. He's made it clear that he doesn't approve of Jack's current lifestyle and this latest stunt…."

He gestured to the newspaper with a pained look. When he turned back to her, she was caught in his gaze. His dark eyes were focused on her with an intensity that was frightening. She couldn't look away.

Ivy squirmed in her seat. Was he trying to torture her? She had no idea what he was getting at but the way he was looking at her, you'd think she single-handedly maneuvered the latest 'stunt,' as he put it. Ivy gripped the edge of her chair to keep calm but she was growing impatient with nerves. She'd already offered to call the newspaper, to try to explain the situation.

"I'm not sure how I can help you," she hedged.

"The only way Brunelli will move forward with this is if I can convince him that Jack has changed. That he's a new man."

There was a brief pause and Ivy wondered if she was supposed to know what he was getting at. She found herself holding her breath as she waited for him to continue but he was either extremely fond of awkward silences or was waiting for her to respond. His eyes were studying her expression though his face was a polite mask, no emotions to be found. He was waiting for a reaction of some sort, that much was clear, but she had no idea where this was heading—only that it couldn't be good.

"Okaaay…" she stalled.

Silence broken, Daniel stood and moved to the front of the desk so he was looming over her. He crossed his arms in front of his chest and fixed his eyes on her. "You see, Brunelli doesn't want to get into bed with someone who's 'not faithful in his private life'—those are his words not mine," Daniel said.

Judging by his smirk, it was clear that this man didn't put much stock in Brunelli's beliefs or his old-fashioned values.

She blinked up at him in the silence that followed. "So, what do you want from me?"

Daniel's laugh took her by surprise. It was a deep rumble that Ivy could feel all the way to her toes. Her breath caught in her throat at the genuine smile that caused his eyes to crinkle and made him seem less intimidating but far more dangerous.

"You're a straight shooter, Ivy. I like that."

She wished his words of approval didn't affect her but she couldn't deny the warm glow that spread through her chest and left her slightly breathless.

He looked her straight in the eye. "I want you to go along with a lie, Ivy. I want you to tell the world that you and Jack are engaged and I want you to play the part of the happy fiancée until this deal is signed."

Ivy found herself staring up at Daniel and for the life of her she was unable to come up with any words. Her brain had turned to mush in her shock and she had the odd sensation that time stood still. The hum of the air-conditioner was temporarily washed out by the sound of her own heartbeat in her ears.

Daniel was eyeing her warily, his gaze fixed on her, and for a moment she thought she saw a hint of concern in his eyes. Those dark eyes that still held her captive.

He was gorgeous. Now was not the time to be thinking about this man's sex appeal, but there it was. Her heart was racing and she was no longer certain if that was due to shock or sexual attraction.

Focus, Ivy. This man wanted her to lie for him—about her entire life.

His voice startled her back to the moment. "I can see my proposition has taken you by surprise." He relaxed his intimidating stance and leaned against the desk with his hands in his pockets as though they were discussing the weather and not her life. "Don't get me wrong, we are not asking you to do anything illegal or anything that would jeopardize your values. You will be handsomely rewarded in return—my investors and I are more than willing to ensure that you are very comfortable financially in return for this favor."

"Other than lie." The words slipped out of her mouth.

Her words put a dent in Daniel's perfectly poised sales pitch. She couldn't help it. Her mother's face loomed in her mind's eye at the mere thought of lying. Her parents had thoroughly ingrained their children with the need to tell the truth, the whole truth, and nothing but the truth.

He paused and raised his brows in polite inquiry. "I'm sorry?"

She cleared her throat. "I said 'other than lie'. You said 'we're not asking you to do anything that would jeopardize your values.' And I said 'other than lie.'"

Oh Lord, she was babbling. She was repeating their conversation like a court reporter. His forehead wrinkled as if in thought for a moment but again she couldn't tell if he was amused or annoyed. Or both.

"Yes, you have a point there. I'm sure lying to your friends and family will not be pleasant but unfortunately, we can't afford to take any chances on anyone slipping up. It would be more difficult for you as well if the truth were to come out. It would not paint you in a flattering light, I'm afraid."

Panic made Ivy's heart rate accelerate. He was talking as though she'd already agreed to go along with this stunt. She shook her head. "I'm sorry, Daniel, but I'm really not a very good liar and I'm not much of an actress. I don't think I could pull it off."

"Unfortunately for us, we don't have much of a choice in who will play the lead in this particular farce." He gestured toward the newspaper. "But you will have a team of people at your beck and call to help you—I am absolutely positive you will get through this little façade with flying colors."

Ivy bristled at his know-it-all tone. Was he really trying to steamroll her into telling a life-altering lie just because it was convenient for him? He wasn't even pretending to frame it as a question—as though it was understood that she would comply.

"Do people always do what you say?" she snapped.

The charming smile faltered. It was slight but she caught it. His perfectly poised demeanor slipped—just for an instant, but it was enough to give Ivy a sense of triumph. She had a feeling that Daniel Gladwell was rarely taken by surprise.

He recovered quickly though and his answer was brutally honest. "Yes, Miss Sinclair. They typically do." *If they know what's good for them.* He didn't say the words but he didn't have to.

Gone was the polite smile and Ivy found herself face to face with Daniel Gladwell, the ruthless business tycoon. His jaw clenched and his eyes hardened, holding her captive yet again in a disarmingly direct glare. He looked like a gladiator ready for battle. The look he gave her was so intense, she swallowed her clever retort—this was not a man to mess with.

"Honestly, Mr. Gladwell, I'd really rather go back my job—"

"Your job will not be waiting for you should you refuse my offer." He stood straight and moved to stand behind the desk. His tone was cool and collected, at odds with the harsh words.

She tried to ignore the uncomfortable sting of unshed tears as his words sank in. She couldn't go back to being unemployed. She'd worked so hard to get where she was. She couldn't start over. And she couldn't go home. Bad investments and a housing market collapse had left her parents teetering on the edge of bankruptcy at an age when they should be planning for retirement. If she lost her job they'd feel compelled to help her but they could barely help themselves.

"That's not fair, you can't do that." Ivy's voice shook. She swallowed and tried again. "The hotel has no reason to dismiss me. I've been a great employee. Ask anyone, ask Mr. Webster."

"It's not a matter of how well you've done your job, Miss Sinclair. The hotel can't keep someone on who acts irresponsibly with the hotel guests. Not to mention, employees here are expected to be team players."

"I am responsible. And I *am* a team player." She tried to keep the tremor out of her voice. She felt like she was on the wrong end of a steamroller. She had to regain control.

She tilted her chin up and straightened her shoulders. Who did he think he was to come to her place of work and threaten her job? Maybe Franklin wasn't in her corner, but there had to be people above him.

Standing, she faced Daniel who had returned to his seat behind the desk. "You can't fire me, Mr. Gladwell. I'm sure Mr. Webster doesn't even have the final say and you have *no* say in the matter so—"

Daniel cut off her tirade before she could even gain steam. "Actually I do have quite a bit of say. My company is the majority owner of this hotel."

His words were like a punch in the gut. Her mind struggled to make sense of this new information. It couldn't be possible—could it? Maybe he was kidding. But even as she thought it, she dismissed it. The man before her clearly didn't have a sense of humor. She stared at him with wide eyes, trying to think of something to say, but she was rendered speechless. She flopped back in her seat like a deflated balloon.

With astonishing speed his cold businesslike demeanor was once again replaced by the charming smile that Ivy was beginning to know well. It was the smile of a predator before it ate its prey. "Listen, Ivy, it doesn't have to be this way. I don't want to lose you as an employee. But I also can't allow yesterday's incident to ruin a multi-billion dollar deal that I've been working on for the past two years. You can understand that, can't you?"

Ivy just stared back at him. Her mind was racing as she considered her options. She could try her luck in an unemployment office once again and pray that she'd find a new position before she lost everything. She could go back home and try to find a job there—but no, that wasn't an option. The job market in her hometown was far worse than the city and she couldn't allow her parents to help her.

"How much?" she asked. "How much would you pay me if I go along with this?"

For a moment she thought he was ignoring her. He picked up a pen and jotted something down on a piece of paper. He pushed it her way and when she picked it up, a series of zeros stared back at her. The six-figure number took her breath away. That was enough to pay her rent for the year and still have plenty left over to help her parents.

"And of course you'll get a promotion, which comes with a raise," Daniel added.

"I don't want a promotion if I haven't earned one," Ivy said, sitting up straight. She may be desperate for money, but she still had some morals.

She thought she saw a hint of a genuine smile again. Good Lord, this man's lips were hypnotic.

"On the contrary, Miss Sinclair. I've had a long talk with Franklin and it seems you have been long overdue for the promotion. I plan to have a talk with him about that." His look of disapproval actually made Ivy nervous on Franklin's behalf.

"So, do I take it we have a deal?"

Ivy swallowed down the feeling that she was taking a leap off of a high dive without checking to see if there was water below.

"We have a deal."

Meet the Author

Maggie Dallen is a huge fan of happily-ever-afters. She writes contemporary and YA romance and has been known to rewrite the endings to classic love stories to ensure that they end on a happy note. In Maggie's version, Ingrid Bergman does not get on the plane. She lives in Northern California and works at a yarn store to support her knitting addiction. For more info please visit maggiedallen.com.

Follow her on Twitter @Mag_Dallen.
Or connect with her on Facebook.

www.ingramcontent.com/pod-product-compliance
Lightning Source LLC
Chambersburg PA
CBHW050750250626
47155CB00005B/2006